Not Taken Series: Book One

Innocence Taken

Trigger Warning

If you are sensitive to obscene language, graphic descriptions of explicit sex acts, use of language describing bodies that is not anatomical and is degrading, dirty dialogue between despicable and disgusting characters, please do not read any further. This book will upset you and you will be offended.

If you are suffering from any form of physical, mental, verbal, or sexual abuse, or suffer PTSD from such abuse or other types of violence or harm, please, shut this book. It will trigger you throughout.

The topic of this book is trafficking of human beings for sexual use and grooming of people from childhood to be used for sex acts.

Terry Ulick
Author

Author's Notes

Born into a family running from the law, my grandfather was a drug dealer and sex trafficker in the Ukraine. I know life in the dark recesses of society. Predators often find less risk doing their deeds in places where people are afraid of the law or have lost all hope for a better life.

In this book, I show how the need to escape from poverty leads young women to respond to offers for being a model. I was a glamour photographer most of my life. For me, it was about showing the beauty of women, and it is wonderful to show the person inside a body, not just their form. Sadly, it can be the opposite. The lure of money, travel, success, and meeting rich men has a strong appeal to young women, and also their mothers. Predators have learned that an audition or a casting call will bring trusting, hopeful young women and underage girls right to their door. Although some may be legitimate, most are not.

Some are simply to sell photo packages or courses on how to model. The women will never see a job, and they will be exploited. Many are lured to pose for sex acts and told that using OnlyFans, they can make good money with sex and their body. As bad as that all is, there is a worse fate.

As you read the story ahead, you will experience that fate. Be prepared. It is horrific, real, and is happening right now as you read this. This is not something reported in media, and that is because most media have long been owned by predators who use young children and young women.

The next time you look at a milk carton, see a "missing" poster hanging on a streetlight pole, or hear about some young girl who is a runaway, after reading this book, you will never see those pictures the same way.

Terry Ulick

Chapter One
Downwardly Mobile

Angie grew up in a trailer park once home to a mansion on ten acres torn down long ago. In a town like Aurora, a mecca for meth labs, strip clubs, prostitution and child molesters, the Hunter Mobile Home Estates was at the top of the list of most dangerous places to live.

Surrounded by rusted mobile homes, trailers and pop-ups, what little space there was between each was filled with broken down cars, bent bicycles, broken furniture, shopping carts, ripped clothing, garbage bags and food thrown out of windows left to rot and attract flies and vermin. Outside the ramshackle dwellings were lawn chairs with empty liquor and beer bottles thrown on the ground, empty cigarette packs, rusted imitation Weber kettles to cook on, and endless newspapers and porn magazines scattered everywhere. Next to the working pickups and motorcycles were men who couldn't stand to be inside with their wives, girlfriends or prostitutes who passed out from too much meth or opioids. They smoked weed or crack, sold drugs, got into fights over if they had sex with whoever they lived with or not, and they all leered at pretty young girls like Angie.

As bad as Hunter Estates was, Angie didn't know it was hell on Earth. She was home schooled, as her mother called it. Born in a motel to an illegal immigrant from the Ukraine, Angie didn't have a birth certificate. The state didn't know she existed, so the school district didn't know she was truant since school age. There were kids in the trailer park who went to school, but most were new to the trailer park and still had hopes a deadbeat dad would come to take them to their nice suburban home to meet their just-turned-18 new wife.

Cindy, Angie's mother, referred to herself as an "escort." The men outside would shout out, "Cindy, I got me a twenty! That enough to escort my dick tonight?" as she'd head out each night to earn her living.

Angie grew up watching her put on makeup and revealing outfits and making the trek with her to the thrift shop to buy frilly bras and panties, tight stretch pants, low-cut knit sweaters and lots of half-full bottles of cologne. While Cindy was off working, when she grew big enough, she'd try on Cindy's piles of too-tight clothes, all of them too large for her, and she'd sit in front of a small round mirror to put on makeup and try to be as pretty as her mom. If her mom had a fast night and came home to find her dressed in her clothes and her face covered with all varieties of colors, she'd tell Angie she looked amazing, then go to her bed, fall down and was out cold.

Having just turned 16, she hated going out of the mobile home. All of the resident bikers, truck drivers and drug dealers kept asking her to come to their place to get high and have sex. Anytime she walked out, the dealer next door was always there, and he always said the same thing.

"Hey, Angie. When you goin' give me some? I got plenty here for you, and we can snort some coke. Hey, that's a good deal for ya!"

Passing the drug dealer, the next trailer was home to a pimp. She prayed each time she'd go out he'd be off somewhere selling his girls as he always was on her.

"You be one fine thing… look at that sweet ass o' yours. Make me some good money with that sweet thang. Give you good cut, take care o' you too. Let you suck my dick for nothin', so come have some now an' tell Marvin you love it."

Cindy had warned her to ignore the men. They wanted something for nothing, and she had something that should never be given away free.

"They're the type that'll use you and lose you. Use you up and move on after they had you."

Cindy knew her mother was an escort. She read all about it in *Cosmo* and *Allure*. They said that it could be a fun side hustle, but they also had articles about how to please a man with blowjobs and remain a virgin. Although she hated the articles, she loved the ads. Models in the ads for cosmetics and clothes were all young and pretty. They didn't wear stuff from the thrift store, and they had classy makeup and she dreamed of looking just like them to be in the ads in those magazines.

Chapter Two
Chores

Hoping to avoid the propositions and comments from the men throughout the trailer park, Angie would get up to go shopping at 6:00 in the morning when the Jewel, the closest grocery store, opened. Her biggest chore was to go there and buy groceries each morning. She learned that nobody living in the trailer park was up that early. Most had just crashed on some stained mattress or sofa or were in jail. Up at 5:30, she'd get dressed and take a folding cart she had found in a junk pile to lug groceries back from the store.

Shopping each day, it was because they didn't have a refrigerator that worked. They had one, but she couldn't recall it ever being on or getting cold when plugged in. Along with the groceries she'd buy a 99-cent bag of ice to put in the fridge to keep meat or milk cold most of the day. After she dressed, she'd go to her mom's purse to find enough money for her shopping list, then quietly leave, locking the door behind her. The Jewel was six blocks away, and she didn't mind the walk once she found the folding cart. Milk and the ice were heavy, and so were the can goods and jars of cheap spaghetti sauce and peanut butter. Her cart was hard to use when it snowed. At that time of the morning the sidewalks weren't shoveled and many times she'd walk in the street as it was usually plowed.

Along with groceries for the day, she'd buy the local newspaper, the *Aurora Light,* and read it until her mother got up. Looking for sales at local stores, she would read the want ads and tried to find any jobs that would hire a 16-year-old. There were a few for after-school help, and those wanted someone with a car and required references. She knew the pimp or dealers were not the references they would consider good, so she kept hoping a simple no-skill-required job would show up. She'd also check the bulletin board at the Jewel, and there were postcards there for jobs sometimes, but mostly ones selling old cars or puppies. Some were pictures of missing children, most often girls her age or younger. She often saw the same pictures on flyers taped to light poles or in store windows. They were pretty with large smiles, and she felt bad for them. She thought they must have gotten tired of living with a pimp dad or hooker mom and run away.

Having just turned 16 on April 14th, Cindy felt sad that Angie had to buy her own birthday cake at the Jewel, but she had managed to get her a card and a nice gift. She decided to stay home as late as possible that night and have a nice dinner she cooked and the two could spend time together.

"Mom, you're cooking? I can do it."

"Angie, it's your birthday. I was going to make a cake for you, but I see you bought one. I'm sorry, sweetie. That's not fair to buy your own. It's pretty, though. I'm making your favorite, so just you take it easy and watch some TV while I get it all done."

Looking, it was her favorite. She had bought hamburger and they had sauce and noodles. There was Parmesan cheese left, so it was spaghetti and meatballs and it smelled wonderful. She started to take out plates, but her mom told her it was her day and she'd take care of it. She saw her mom was enjoying doing all the dinner preparation, so she read a magazine on her bed and waited. It didn't take long until her mom called her.

"Angie, all ready! Come sit down."

Cindy had made everything as nice as possible, telling Angie she would do the washing up as well.

"I'm starting late tonight. This is your special day. 16… I can't even remember being 16, but I want you to. I enjoyed cooking all this. I miss it. Maybe if I meet someone nice, we can live someplace better…"

Angie nodded, doubting what she said as she had been saying it for years. They both enjoyed the food, and being together. After eating as much as each could, Cindy cleared the table and put the small cake in front of Angie and had managed to find candles for it, excited as she lit them.

"Angie, I know it seems silly, but make a wish when you blow them out. Someday one of your wishes has to come true!"

Blowing the 17 candles out with one breath, 16 were for each year, the 17th for good luck. Angie watched her mom slice the cake, and getting up, Cindy told her to stay sitting, there was more. Angie knew she usually had some little gift for her and guessed that was what she referred to. Cindy went away for less then a minute then returned with a box she had hid. Wrapped nicely, it had a card envelope under a ribbon on it.

"Mom, I think this is the biggest birthday box ever… Wow!"

Pulling the card from under the ribbon, she opened it, and as she read it she started to tear up. She read it out loud while Cindy watched.

"My Little Girl Is Growing Up… I've watched you grow and grow, and I want you to always know, no matter how tall you grow to be, you'll always be a little girl, to me."

Under the verse was a big hand-drawn heart and, "Love, Mom."

After they each cried and looked at each other, Angie started pulling off the wrapping paper and was surprised to see the box was from Macy's. She first thought it was just a box her mom had found outside, but it looked new and clean. As she opened it, there was white tissue paper, and under it was a black dress. Jumping up, Angie held it in front of her, stunned as it was unexpected. It was a slim classic black dress, sleeveless, scoop collar, and it looked to be a perfect fit.

                                                      Innocence Taken

"Mom, this is like, well… new. Is this actually from Macy's?"

"Sure is! No thrift store dress for you today. Hey, put it on. Let's see it on you!"

Running to the back of the trailer, she pulled off her jeans and sweater, leaving the tag in place as she pulled the dress on. It was a wonderful fit, and she turned and turned as she looked at herself in the closet door mirror. Running back to the kitchen, she stopped in front of Cindy, then did simple model poses showing the dress from the front, side, and back. Cindy looked with her mouth open, amazed at her little girl.

"Angie, you're just the prettiest thing I've ever seen. Why, you look like Audrey Hepburn in that! And it's such a sweet fit. You know, I have that string of cheap pearls, and they'd go perfect with it. Oh, you're going to be a looker. What am I saying? You *are* a looker!"

Hugging Cindy, she said she wasn't going to risk getting it mussed and went back to change and hang it up, putting it in a clear plastic bag from the cleaners. She smiled at it in the closet. It was the nicest gift she had ever received.

Getting back to the kitchen, Cindy was waiting for her and had poured some store-brand cola for them both.

"Angie, I've been thinking. We both know I haven't done too well. I can't have a real job, and with what I do… well, finding a decent man hasn't happened. I've hit bottom and here we are. But you… don't you be like me. Your pretty as a peach, and you sure are sweet. We both know you'll never have a good life here in this hellhole. Not one man here worth talking to. Scum of the Earth. And their boys? Even worse. Bad dads raise them to be even worse than they are. Now, I know it's hard not having schooling or even the books. Maybe I'll find a way to get you a birth certificate and you can get a social security card in a year or two. Do it now, and social workers will want to know about you not being in school and all. But maybe there's ways to make something of yourself right now."

Angie was amazed as nothing about any of the things Cindy said had ever been talked about. She asked her what she could possibly do.

"First off, you're never going to do what I do, understand?"

Angie nodded, promising her she understood, and wouldn't. Cindy gave her a serious nod.

"Don't ever do that — no matter how hard things get. So, I've been thinking about it. I saw a sign tacked up in a large apartment building I work. It had little tear-off phone numbers and I have one. It's something I think you could do and make good money doing it."

Looking puzzled, Angie asked, "What, momma?"

"It said there was a tryout for girls your age to audition to be models. Said the pay was tops, and it was for 14 to 18s, no experience required and if you have the right look, they'd train you. It's one of the reasons for your gift. It said to tryout, wear a simple black dress. It's more than a dress, honey. I hope it's for your future. A good job doing something you can be proud of."

Jumping up and hugging Cindy, she was crying and excited at the same time. She had been looking in the magazines and thinking how wonderful it would be to be a fashion model, then as if knowing what she was dreaming of, her mom was showing she may be able to become a model, or at least get a start.

"Mom, do you really think I stand a chance? Am I pretty enough?"

Cindy looked at her and thought to herself, "Too pretty." She nodded happily as she looked at her. Angie was right out of a magazine. Tall for her age, thin, lovely shape, long legs, breasts small but enough there to notice, and most of all, her face was much like Audrey Hepburn's. Large cheekbones, big eyes, perfect lips and smile, and long dark brown hair. She had a certain style and grace when she walked. Cindy lived in constant fear of her being dragged into some trailer and raped. Angie was too pretty to be safe if they stayed living like they did with all the sick men hanging around. She had noticed how the men had begun staying near their mobile home more than ever recently, and she had heard them talking about Angie when they weren't looking her way. Things had to change. Angie would only grow more beautiful as she grew up. The world wasn't a safe place for a beautiful girl. And of all the places in the world, she thought Aurora and the Hunter Mobile Home Estates was the least safe place for Angie.

Chapter Three
Call, Girl

Planning on spending the next day getting up early as usual, while shopping Angie had saved some money on groceries by only buying store brands and cutting corners with produce, so she had enough to visit the cosmetic aisle. Looking for the kind of eyeliner and lipstick she saw that models in magazines were wearing, if she was going to audition to be a model, she needed to look up to date. Not used to looking at store-priced products, she quickly learned that the same color of lipstick could be $18 for one brand, or $4 for another. With popular colors, most all brands had them. Finding all she needed totaled under $10.

Her next stop was to look at shampoo. She had been using bar soap from a dollar store and wanted something to make her hair shine and have body. After reading a dozen labels making all kinds of promises, she found a silky body-building conditioner from Suave for $1.99. The final item was a disposable razor and the store brand for a pack of three was $1.59. Smiling, she had all she needed and had enough to go back for some carrots.

That morning she checked the bulletin board where the shopping carts were held. Looking, there was the flyer her mother had seen. Growing excited, she was glad to find it so she could read the details. Moving herself to get a close look, she read every word with anticipation.

Looking for the Next Top Model

Runaway Elite is looking for stylish, sophisticated young women aged 14-18 to become top runway fashion models. If you dream of making it big in the world of fashion, are right out of the pages of Vogue, we're looking for you. If you can strut, stride, turn, look at judges and let them know with one look that you're the next big star, this is your once-in-a-lifetime chance.

Modeling experience is not necessary. We like to work with fresh talent. We train you the right way, and our team will develop your "look," style you, teach you to walk and show your attitude.

We have clients waiting, and they're looking for fresh new talent. That may be you!

Top models make big money, travel the world, meet superstars, and top models start their success with Runaway Elite.

If you're young, have a body that shouts out, "I'm a Cover Girl!" then we want to meet with you. Now!

We'll be in town for one week at the Willow Tree Suites. Come dressed to impress. A simple black dress is ideal. Call the number below and set up your audition. We can't wait to have you!

On the side of the flyer, from top to bottom, was a tall, thin, slinky young girl in a tight club dress showing lots of attitude. Below, some of the tear-off phone numbers had been taken, and that made Angie anxious as she hoped there were still appointments available.

Rushing home, she made it just before the scary men made their way to their lawn chairs. After putting things away, she went to the landline they had in the back room and called the number. After two rings, they answered the phone.

"Runaway. We're looking for new talent. Are you the one?"

It sounded like a girl her age, and that made her comfortable.

"I hope so. I'd like to audition like it says on your flyer, the one in stores."

"Like, for sure, if you qualify. Are you, like, in your teens?"

"I turned 16 yesterday."

"Wow, that's awesome. Happy B-day! Are you like… drop dead hot?"

"Well, that's what I've been told."

"Skinny? I mean, like, really skinny?"

"I'm pretty thin. Size 0. So, yes."

"That's awesome. How tall?

"Five eight, but because I'm really thin, I look even taller."

"Are you, like, gorgeous?"

"I'm Ukrainian. You know, just like models from there all look. High cheekbones and stuff."

"Super. Now, is this your first time, I mean, like, have you modeled before?"

"First time."

"Great. So, we start by having you come in. We look you over, and if you're hot, we have you do a test modeling session. Walk up and down like you're on a runway. We'll take a video and some stills and put you in different outfits and stuff. If you're a 0 we have lots to put you in. After that, we talk to you and give you an idea of what type of work you'd be good for. We do all kinds of stuff."

"Wow, that's a lot of things. I'm a bit nervous as I've never modeled before. How many people will I be doing all that with. I mean, do you group by age, or size?"

"Well, when you come in we decide right away if you're what we want, so that weeds out most who show up. It's not group. It's one at a time. Don't worry, we have ways to make you feel really comfortable. We can do it tomorrow. How's noon sound?"

Angie said that sounded great, then the girl asked for all of her basic information. As she hung up the phone she started jumping up and down, turning in circles. She couldn't believe she had an appointment. She went and opened her new cosmetics and began learning how to make herself look hot.

After a lot of experimenting, she went heavy with everything like so many models in the magazines did. After a lot of lipstick, blush, mascara, and making her eyebrows large as she could, she looked in the mirror and immediately said to herself, "I look like a slut!"

Washing it all off, she hoped that wasn't the look they were hoping for.

Chapter Four
Not Past Anything

Going to the closet, considering the dress had been folded in the box and would show fold lines, she turned the hot water on in the shower to steam it. Carefully cutting the tags off, she put them in a small pencil box she bought at Jewel, and she looked at other items in the box while the dress was relaxing in the hot steam of the shower.

The box didn't contain much, but what was there was precious to her. At the bottom was a picture of her when just born that her uncle had taken of her and her mother. Not born in a hospital, the picture was taken in a motel room, and her mother look joyous holding her. It was a bittersweet memory for her mother as Jake, her brother, died soon after she was born. He committed suicide in the same motel where the picture was taken. Cindy had only told her the full story about Jake a year prior, and she understood why she waited until she was old enough to hear it. Jake, and her mother, had both been sexually abused as young children. Jake had it the worst, and she prayed for him each night.

While Angie was growing up, Cindy never spoke about her parents. Angie was always curious about her grandparents. When Cindy finally told her what happened to Jake, she also told her about them. It was fresh in her mind.

"Sweetie, I'm so glad you never met them. I still shake and get sick thinking about them, but I'm doing okay right now. I decided to tell you all this stuff I have kept from you because you need to know."

"Mom, don't tell me if it makes you sick!"

"I'm okay, Angie. I'm okay. Maybe it will help getting it all out of my system. Well, you know we're Ukrainian and we speak it. I'm glad I taught you English while real little, growing up. You speak it perfectly. We're here in the US, so you had to know how. So, my parents were really messed up. I mean, bad people. Really bad. My father… Oh, he was a monster no matter which way you turned him. You know all that low life that's hanging around all the time outside? Yeah. Well, they're saints compared to him."

"Mom! You mean he hurt you guys?"

"He hurt everyone. See, they grew up there when it was communist, and people didn't like it and didn't even have enough to eat and all. My dad… He learned when he was really young how to make money doing terrible things. He didn't get in trouble as he took care of the commie officials. Over there, you did a job they told you to do, you lived in a crummy flat they put people in, and you ate what they handed you. No extra money, no TV, nothing. My dad worked for one of the Commie officials as a handyman. He saw how people would come and give the commie man things. Gifts. And women. The big shot loved getting young girls to, well, have sex with. And the ones giving him those poor little girls? In exchange, they had money, cars, a nice place to live."

"Mom… Didn't people report him? I mean, that's like really bad."

"People who did ended up in a cold prison for life. Or shot. No, it was a bad place. When my dad was just about 19, he decided he wanted money and a car and he saw how it all worked. So, he became a pimp. Talked young women into living a bit better by whoring themselves out. It's the same everywhere. A woman, she either gets lucky and marries a decent man, or if she's broke, she ends up whoring herself out. He told us women were happy to get some extra food or some clothes if they did what he told them to. That was bad enough, but he had no trouble hurting people. He'd kill other pimps, beat up a girl who backed out… He was ruthless and everyone feared him. He met my mom looking for girls to whore out. He saw her and she was so beautiful, he decided to keep her for himself. I still don't know if they got married."

"She was going to be a hooker?"

"Yep, she was. She didn't have much of a choice. The local police brought her in, but not because she did anything. Her parents were dead, and she was alone. The police took her so they could rape her. That's the kind of thing that went on. They did that just as my dad decided to make her his own girl. He was providing girls to the Commie governor, and he could get away with anything. He found out the police took her, so he went to the police station and killed them all. Shot them in the head and walked out with my mother. Never heard a word about it. He was free to do what he wanted."

"Mom! Murdered them, just like that? He was that bad?"

"Angie, that was nothing. He did so much more. With the money he made from providing poor girls to the Commie officials, he learned how much more he could make selling drugs. That's when things got way beyond bad, and that started after Jake and I were born. I grew up thinking drugs were no big deal. He started by taking his money and buying drugs, then selling it to the officials. They used it to drug up girls, then he started doing that to the girls to keep them in line. Once someone's hooked on what he'd give them… heroin, they were his. So, he ended up being a pimp and a drug czar and he killed anyone who tried to horn in on his territory. I have no idea how many. He'd just come home and talk to my mom and would say he killed some small-time pimp or dealer. She seemed excited by it. She was right there by his side. She thought he was some powerful guy and she had furs and jewelry. She didn't have a problem with it."

"Wow, mom. I had no idea. And you grew up around all of that?"

"Sweetie, we didn't know better and thought that was just how things were. We were used to mounds of heroin on the dining room table, girls running around naked. He was having sex with them in the house for us to see, and my mother didn't care. It was business. He'd tell her he had to test the merchandise. Imagine that. Calling some girl he had hooked on drugs merchandise."

"But, mom… You said he was really bad to you and Jake. If he did that, you mean he did that kind of stuff to you guys too?"

"This is really hard to talk about, but it'll explain a lot of things and you're old enough to know. See, my dad started using his own drugs. The heroin. People who use that? They're crazy. One minute he'd be nice, the next minute he'd be in a rage and shooting at people. He tried to get my mother on it too, but thank Mary, she said she had to keep sane and take care of business, so she said she never did any of it. I can't be sure. That's when we were about… well, Jake was 13, and I was about 11. One day, I see my father passed out and all wet on the couch, and Jake ran to our room all wet and crying. Oh, this is harder than I thought it would be… Okay, okay… I can do it. I can."

"Mom, you don't have to. I know you mean he was a real bad man, but you got away from him."

"Angie, not soon enough. Well, I went after Jake, and he was like, well, in shock. I couldn't get him to talk for a few hours. I kept rubbing him and telling him it was me, and he was okay with me. When he could finally talk, he told me our dad raped him. He was so messed up and crazy from the drugs and the girls, and I guess he lost his mind. He grabbed poor Jakey and bent him over a big tank of water… Oh, it's something I heard him cry about so many times… My dad put his head in it, and pulled down his pants and went at him. You know, from behind. That messed Jake up forever. And he kept doing it to him…"

"Oh, mom! Poor uncle Jake. I can't… I mean, like, I can't understand all this. Why? And why put his head underwater and all?"

"I couldn't figure it out back then either. I thought it was to tell Jake he'd drown him if he didn't let him do him like that. But…

ah, no… no, it wasn't that. One day I asked Jake if he was still dunking him in the tank, and he just looked at me. Oh, God, he was so sad… He looked at me and said that nobody could hear him screaming with his head in the water. I went and threw up. I couldn't believe it. No, I really couldn't believe it, and I knew my mom knew. Oh, she knew. She knew…"

"Mom, stop. Take a while to calm down… Maybe lay down, okay?"

Angie saw the look on her mother's face, thinking it must feel the same for her as the day Jake told her. She was reliving the trauma. Just hearing it was a nightmare, so she could only imagine what her mother must have felt. And her uncle… she realized he had a reason for drinking and using drugs and then one day, killing himself. How could anyone be okay after going through all that?

She sat on her bed, crying for her mother, crying for Jake. After an hour, Cindy called for her to come sit so she can finish telling her things she needed to know. She didn't want to hear more, but knew it was important to her mother. She said it would explain why things were the way they were now. She went and joined her mother in the little kitchenette, and her mom had a large bottle of root beer and glasses for them.

"That sleep helped some. Now, all I can do is just get this out. Just say it, okay? It's important for you to know."

"Okay, mom. I know it's hard for you, but I won't react like I did before. I'll listen, okay?"

"It's going to be hard to hear. Well, my mom finally admitted to me she knew about Jakey, and she wasn't okay with what my dad was doing. They'd fight when he was rational, and he would knock her around real bad. Jakey? He was afraid he'd kill him if he fought back. It was, well, when he was around 14, and I just started getting my period and it was early. 12, I'm sure. After a big fight

Innocence Taken

between my dad and my mom, she was knocked out because she started beating on him and he punched her. Jakey loved mom, so he was trying to stop him. He smacked him and sent him flying. I can still see him hit the stove and he just fell to the floor. I was watching, shouting for it all to stop. Then, my dad looked at me. He was crazy high on drugs. He had left me alone until then, but when he looked at me? Oh, that's a look I pray you never see. He didn't care mom and Jakey were knocked out. He just walked up to me, grabbed me, dragged me to my bed, and raped me."

Shaking from remembering the look on her mother's face as she told her what her grandfather had done, she had a hard time thinking of what she was told next. She sat, shaking, tears pouring out of her eyes, and that reminded her to go turn off the hot water. She didn't want to damage her new dress. It was almost wet with dampness, but it looked smooth and as if it had been sent to the cleaners. Leaving it to dry in the shower, she went back to her memory box and held the picture of her and her mother when she was born. The meaning of all she had just been told washed over her. Clutching it, she went to sit with her mother

"Angie, this is the hardest part. He raped me, that one time. He left me there, and I was so afraid. I thought, just like Jakey, he'd kill me if I tried to stop him. He filled me up, I'll say that for him. He was virile, alright. I was laying there, and I heard him slam the door and he went out. After a bit, my mother was back up, and she got Jakey up too. She came, looked at me, and she saw his semen ooze out of me, and she knew what he had done to me. I saw her face. I'll never forget it. That look. She cleaned me up, telling me he'd never do anything to me or Jakey ever again. My dad, he was gone for days at a time. It was near morning. My mom, she was near as hard as my father. She got a bag, gathered all his drugs, put all his money in another bag and put it in a suitcase along with our clothes, and then she went and found his guns. She put them all in there too. She said we were going to leave in a while, but she had something to do first…"

"Oh, God, mom! He raped you! And you were just 12! How did you survive that? How could you be okay after that?"

"I've never been okay with that. No, you never get over that. They call it PTSD. I can't get it out of my mind. Well, how did I survive? Mom took care of it real quick. She took a kitchen chair and put it far back from the front door. She just sat there and told us to be dressed as we'd be going when my father got back. She sat there, in the dark. We hid. Then, it got light as it was pretty much noon, and we heard stumbling outside, so it was him coming home. He opened the front door, then we heard an explosion. My mom was sitting there with his biggest gun. A monster of a thing. He came through the door, and she shot him in the chest, and he flew back against the door he just closed. A minute went by, then we heard mom ask him if he wanted to fuck me again. Then another explosion. She shot him in the face. She came and got us, and we had to walk over him with the bags to get out. I won't tell you what that looked like, but I saw Jakey spit where his face used to be…"

"But mom! Weren't you and Jakey glad she stopped him? I mean it was horrible to see that, but he couldn't hurt you anymore…"

Thinking of the picture of her as a newborn, Angie once thought it was a happy picture. It was, in a way, but it had a new meaning after she heard the rest of the story. She sat crying thinking of how her mother looked at her as she finished telling what happened.

"Angie, sometimes, like a memory, that hurt keeps happening. I'll tell you what we did, first. My mom, she went to some town in the car and found some other drug dealer, and she wanted to sell him the drugs. Showing up with us, and the drugs, he said, 'You bring me drugs. Nice of you. You think I give money?' He said she was foolish woman… the way you say it in Ukrainian. He said, 'I take drugs, you go fuck yourself.' As he laughed, my mother took the gun from her purse and shot him. He was dead. She took his money, her drugs, and his drugs too. She got back in the car, then went to another town and that time she held the gun out pointed to that drug dealer's head and said, 'Money you give, drugs I give, yes?' The man knew she'd kill him, so she followed him to where he hid his money, and he bought the drugs. After that, we drove without stopping. She gave lots of money at each checkpoint and we made it out of there. Then she paid someone for fake papers and passports, and we got on a plane and came here. She bought this mobile home."

"Mom! Oh my God! That's worse than in any movie! Weren't you scared out of your mind? I mean, guns and sneaking out of the country? What if you got arrested?"

"No, she wasn't worried. Money got anyone out. She had the gun on her lap, and the border guards took the money, not a bullet. So, before we lived here, we were in a dive motel and that's where you were born. That's the part where I meant my father did more than rape me. Angie, this part isn't something I'm sad about. He did more than rape me. He got me pregnant. That's how I had you."

Putting the photo down, she sat, numb. Her mother had been raped by her father, he got her pregnant, and her father was her grandfather too. She was her mother's sister, and daughter. It was too much to think about, and she shook herself. She was okay, healthy, and her mother loved her and never hurt her in any way. Then, she looked at the picture of Jakey. That was different. That was much worse. She remembered all the rest.

After talking about how she was born, her mother told her she was what saved her. She was her own little Aurora. A bright light. She thought about how her mother's face changed when she asked about her mom, and Jake. It was the saddest part of all of it.

"Well, you need to understand we were — well, I still am — illegal immigrants. We had fake papers, and she didn't want us to get deported back. So, she bought us this place, and we laid low. You were born in a motel just before she bought this from some weird guy for cash. We were living in that crummy motel, and then we moved here. Well, I did. She had it all bought, and I took you here in a cab, and they were getting things packed at the motel. Now, this is so important. I survived and had you, and I was so happy to have my little malenka! I got better. Jakey? He got worse. He just kept thinking about how our mom let his dad do that to him over and over. She only shot him and escaped because of me being raped. He would yell at her that she didn't stop his dad from hurting him, but she stopped him to save me. He was never mad at me about it. Never. We both know what happened. So, I was waiting, and he came back, but not my mom. He just walked in, put down a revolver, and said he told her he'd shoot her if he ever saw her again. He was really as screwed up as our dad at that point, and I knew he had been doing drugs once we got here, just like his dad. Mom knew it too, and she took him seriously. I saw the look on his face that night. I never saw her again, but I did get a letter from her, and she had managed to move back to the Ukraine. She said all she knew was selling drugs and whoring out girls, but she'd deal like our dad had done, and she'd do alright. She said she'd send me her phone number soon, and she did. I never called her, no matter how poor we were. I don't want that sick money, but I kept the number just in case. So, with her gone, it was just Jakey, you, and me."

"Mom! Mom! I can't believe it!"

"I think you can figure it out now. Why he killed himself. He made sure you and I were okay. He gave me all our things, the paper title to this place, all the money he had found in her suitcase, though she had more hid, I'm sure. She saw how messed up he was, and she was smart and wasn't going to have him treat her like our dad had. That's what we've been living on. He said never let anyone know who we were, ever. Don't send you to school. I couldn't get a respectable job. I knew what he meant. I knew. He knew. Then, he said he thought he forgot a few things at the motel and left, putting the gun in his pocket. He sure forgot it all. He shot himself. I read about it in the papers the next morning. They found a dead boy, no note, no clue who he was. I know it may sound horrible, but he's not suffering anymore. So, I couldn't even get him buried. I still can't even ask what they did with him. I started being an escort. Did some stripping too. No ID needed for any of that. If I die, you were born here. That picture? It's from the motel room. You can tell this story. You'll become a legal citizen. Just, well, not yet, okay?"

Putting the picture back in the pencil box, Angie realized how much her mother had done to protect her. Now, she wanted to protect her from the creeps and drug addicts in the motor court around them. She wanted to get them both away. Go find a job like being a model where she wouldn't stay and get raped by one of the horrible men outside. That's what the dress was about. She looked at the dress again, and she promised herself that she would find a way out of where they were, no matter what it took. Her mother had done everything she could to protect her. Now, she would do the same for her mother. She could explain what a nightmare she'd been through if she found the right person in the immigration office. First, she needed to get a job, and maybe she'd meet some powerful people who could help.

Holding the dress up against herself, she nodded. She would use her looks the way her grandmother used her gun.

Chapter Five
The Runaround

Somehow, looking in her memento box made going to the audition different than her initial excitement of being a model and maybe being in one of the magazines she loved to look at. The audition was now more like her mother getting to America and finding a way to take care of her. She wanted to take care of her mother now. She would find a way to get her foot in the door, make money, become a citizen, and move away from trailers and mobile homes and Aurora. That gave her a look of determination. Looking at herself in the reflection of the bus window as she rode to the audition, she thought it gave her a look of poise and confidence.

Getting off the bus, she brushed her dress off in case anything from the seat had stuck. She stood in front of Willow Tree Suites and saw it was an ordinary motor hotel for business travelers as it was close to the airport. Taking a deep breath, she walked into the lobby and saw a framed board with a hand-written announcement that Runaway Elite Auditions were in Ballroom Two, and it had a crudely drawn arrow pointing the way. The lobby was empty, and that time of day she figured most guests had checked out, and new guests wouldn't arrive until later. The man at the front desk looked at her, not smiling, giving her a long look, checking her out. She imagined he probably lived in the trailer park.

Going into the restroom off the lobby, she checked her makeup and hair, then stood up tall and knew posture would matter. She thought she looked good after a slow bus ride, then left to find Ballroom Two.

There was a sheet of copy paper on a large door with marker writing on it. "Model Auditions" was all it said. Taking a deep breath, she opened the door, went in, a smile on her face. Once inside she saw there was a long table with tacked-on white pleated drapes on the front of it. Behind it sat a woman talking on a cell phone, putting her finger up to indicate she'd be with her in a short time. Nodding, she was surprised. The woman's voice was the one she heard on her call for an appointment, but she wasn't a young teen model type. Guessing the woman was in her late twenties, attractive, she was wearing little makeup and clothes that were not currently in fashion. She wore costume jewelry and was taking notes as she talked to whoever was on the phone, saying much the same she had told her, asking all the same questions in the same teenage valley girl manner. Finally saying goodbye, can't wait to see you, she ended the call and looked up at her.

"You must be Angie. I'm sorry to keep you waiting. So many girls want to try out, I'm on the phone most all the time. Well, let's get things started. Here's a form to fill out. I have all the information you gave me on the phone, so make sure it's all correct. Read it over as it's a model release and an agreement. You just read it and sign it. There's a seating area over there, so bring it back when you're done checking that everything's correct."

Angie looked to where she pointed, and there were three stacking chairs and a small round table to put things on. She was surprised as when the woman talked to her, she talked completely different than when on the phone. She talked like someone from the midwest and sounded much her right age. She was business-like but didn't talk like she did to people calling. She figured using the phony voice made young girls relate better and made them feel comfortable, but it still surprised her.

Going over the form, all her name and address information was correct, and her weight, height and measurements were all filled in. There was an open square saying, "Photo here." Under that was small type that she read carefully.

"I agree to give all rights to my image in photographs or in video for Morozov LLC to use in any manner without limits. I agree that all images in any media format are the property of Morozov LLC and I may not use them unless granted in writing. Any images that I request may or may not be given, and if given, I agree to pay industry standard rates for professional services and production costs. I grant all rights to my likeness for any purpose to Morozov LLC, and hold Morozov LLC harmless for any legal matters arising from its use of my likeness or image, or any form of my direct contact with clients of Morozov LLC."

Under it was a line for a signature, printed name, and date signed. Under that was another block of small print type.

"I hereby authorize Morozov LLC to manage my professional services in any capacity, and to present and represent me in the pursuit of modeling for photography or videos, participation in fashion events including fashion shows, runway appearances, personal modeling for clients, and any activity that will generate income for Morozov LLC. I will accept all work obtained for me by Morozov LLC, and will not work with any other agency, manager, representative, or offer myself for hire for any modeling, personal appearance work, or client-requested activities. All work product will be the property of Morozov LLC, and I release all rights upon signing this agreement. Morozov LLC will make all efforts to obtain work and placing me, and in return for getting me work and representing me in all the above activities, I will be paid 40% of any money paid for my services, work, images, or personal appearances or activities for any activity requested by clients of Morozov LLC. I agree that I can be dismissed from this agreement at any time by Morozov LLC, but I cannot exit or violate the terms of this agreement without surrendering all outstanding money owed to Morozov LLC for my image, or work not done for clients."

Under was the signature line, and then one additional section.

"I, __________________________ , state that I am a US Citizen, and I am of legal age and I signed this agreement willingly, have provided proof of age, and agree to all of the above willingly.

Then, another signature line.

Reading and rereading it all, Angie was confused and unsure of what it all meant. She had never read a legal document, and she had thought she was there to audition for Runaway Elite, not the Morozov LLC. Also, she thought she would have to give the agency a percent of her income, but the agreement took more than half, and it prevented her from doing other modeling if she should find work in addition to what they could. What worried her most was it stating she was of legal age, and able to sign a legal document. She had told the woman she was 16, not 18, and that was not expected. Her heart was beating fast. She was determined to get modeling work, but the agreement was not at all what she had expected. Holding her pen, she decided to ask questions first before signing anything.

Dragging the stacking chair with her, she put it in front of the woman behind the table, saying she had questions. The woman smiled with understanding, and leaned forward.

"Oh, sweetheart, I haven't introduced myself. I'm Jamie. Hi. So, I could see you reading things very carefully, and that's why I asked you to read it thoroughly. So, ask me what needs explaining."

Feeling somewhat relieved that Jamie understood, she relaxed enough to go through her concerns.

"Well, I am really confused about who the agreement is with. I thought this was for Runaway Elite, but it has a person's name all over instead…"

"I understand. Oh, it's all legal things. Runaway Elite is a wonderful name, but it's just the name we use as nobody would understand what or who Morozov is! That's our legal name. The man who owns Runaway Elite. It's the legal name when we do business. Who would know what a Morozov is?"

Scrunching her brow, Angie looked at her.

"I do. It's a Ukrainian name. Is it a Ukrainian company?"

"Why, aren't you smart! No, not Ukie. Russian. It's a Russian company, yes, very perceptive of you. It uses the same name both in Russia and the US. So, a Russian company, and there are tons of foreign companies operating in America. Are you from the Ukraine? Speak it?"

"My mother was from there, and moved here right when I was born, so I was born here. Yes, you know, if you speak Ukrainian, you know Russian, Polish, some others…"

"Why, that is wonderful! We have so much modeling going on in Russia, and for Russian clients here. That gives you so much more opportunity. I can't wait for Vlad to hear that!"

"And, Vlad is?"

"He owns the business. Vladimir Morozov. You'll meet him soon. Now, what next?"

"It says that if I do any pictures or video things, it belongs to him, and I don't even get a say or a copy and things like that. And it seems to be that way for anything I do. I want to say yes or no to work and have copies of my pictures and things. I've read about how models work in *Elle* and *Allure* and places, and they kind of are in control of that."

"Oh, those silly magazines. Get young girls all confused. That's for one or two hot stuff models and even then, I doubt any of that is true. Well, remember, if there's a magazine shoot, or a runway job, you can't just walk in and say hire me. You wouldn't even know they were looking for models. So, we go and meet with people and show your samples and convince them to work with you, make all the deals, handle the contracts and make sure you get paid. Even if we don't get paid, we have to pay you and that comes out of our pocket. And we train you, get a portfolio together. Oh, the list goes on and on. It's a lot of work and it's how we get jobs for you. In exchange, we take our share, pay yours. We do so much you'll never see. Ads in industry magazines, all of that. And we need to be free to use your image where and when we need to. It wouldn't work if we had to ask you each time. And copies of things? Oh, we give you ones that are nice, sure. But once in a while a girl will want tons of them to give to friends, so we say that to keep things like that from happening... And, sometimes, a girl will send our pictures to another modeling agency or post them online to get work elsewhere, and we've done all the hard work!"

"Okay. I understand, and I know I'm just starting out. But the thing that concerns me is that I'm saying I'm of legal age, and I'm not. That would be lying."

"Yes, it is a tricky one. See, since you're signing with this form, you're signing with our company in Russia. In Russia, the legal age is 16. That's why I was so happy hearing you had just turned 16. We wouldn't have you sign it if it wasn't legal. Your pay will come from our bank in Russia, and if you look way on the bottom... see there... I know it's small, but it says Morozov LLC is a wholly-owned subsidiary of Morozov Inc., a Russian Company under the laws of Russia. We are very careful to do things right both in the US and in Russia. Now, anything else?"

Sitting, thinking, she had been given answers that seemed to make sense, and she worried about what would happen if they were not good to work with. She was also determined to get her career started. She figured she could always get out of the agreement but wanted to make sure about that.

"One more thing. It says you can let me go, but if I want to stop, I don't get my money for work I've done. If I'm not happy or have to move, you know, something unexpected, this doesn't seem to be good if that happens."

"Well, that is a very good question. Now, like I said, when you work, we've done a lot of work to get you placed. So, if you leave, we've done so much work, it's a way to make sure we get paid for the work we do for you. Before we make money, you do. It's also a bit of incentive to stay with us once you get well known and other agencies try to hire you away. We'd have done all the work to make them want to hire you, and after we do all that, they lure you away and we can't make money after all we've done. I need to be honest. Look around. Is there any other agency here offering to build your success and invest in you? No. We're the only one doing that. This will help you remember who made you be in demand. We both work hard, so we should both be rewarded."

Sitting back, Angie got the gist of what she was saying, and she wasn't sure, so asked one more question.

"Okay, I think I get it. But I just want to be sure that, well, if I hate being a model, or I get sick or anything that would make it where I want to quit, I can say I need to stop, and I just won't get any more money, but it's not like I would owe you money or be forced to stay working, right?"

"Hmmm. I don't think that would be an issue. We do keep track of money we spend to get your work. Like airfare if a job is somewhere far away. Clothes, model portfolios, runway training. Lots of things, actually. Those come out of your first paychecks, and we take a bit out at a time. If we do all that, and you leave before we can pay all the people who did that for you, well… you would owe it to us, or work it off. We invest in you, big time. Once we do that, you could go to another agency and you have all that, and you will make more money with that training, so it's only fair. But a few jobs and it's all paid for, so that hasn't really ever come up. Well, I think you're one sharp cookie! You asked amazing questions. So, once you sign, then Vlad needs to sign it too. So, if you sign it, I have him meet you, see how you look in front of a camera and things. Then he makes a commitment to you by signing it too. He'll invest in you. So, if you're ready and agree, I'll let him know you're good to go!"

　　　　　　　　　　　　　　　　Innocence Taken

Chapter Six
Speaking the Same Language

Having doubts about the one-sided nature of the agreement, Angie's determination to get her career started was stronger than her doubts. Somehow, it being a Russian company made her think of her grandfather and what she had learned of life and behavior there. Thinking of how they weren't in Russia, they were in the US, she found herself signing all the places on the form. Jamie watched her, smiling, then said she would have a copy for her if Vlad brought her onboard and signed it too.

Getting up, she said she was going to tell Vlad she had signed the agreement and was ready to meet him. Angie grew both excited and nervous. If the company was a good one, it would be the start of a legitimate life and a career. If not, she would have to find a different modeling agency or company who would be interested in her. Aurora wasn't the fashion capital of America, so she wouldn't know where to start if Vlad didn't want to work with her.

Waiting, she started reminding herself she could still back out before they invested any time or money in her. That would only happen if she didn't trust Vlad. She thought of how strange it was that the one job she applied for happened to be for a Russian man, or company, or whatever it all was. As she worried about it all, she heard a voice call to her.

"Angie. Please to come, much time filling out stupid forms, yes?"

She turned and knew the man talking to her was Vlad.

She had expected some older, stocky Russian oligarch with a thick mustache and greased hair. Vlad looked like he had stepped off the cover of a romance novel. Tall, thin, clearly muscle-bound, he wore expensive-looking gray wool slacks, a white shirt opened to mid-chest, tanned, and his face was handsome in every way. High cheekbones, classic slightly slanted eyes like Russians who descended from Mongolia often had, a soft smile, deep green eyes, and his hair was brown with light streaks as if he had spent too much time in the sun. It was long, wavy, worn back and it cascaded over his white collar. He had a distinct Russian accent, and that made his appeal stronger in her mind. She thought if anyone should be modeling, it should be him. He stood, casual, smiling, waiting.

Getting up, she held out her hand and for a moment expected him to kiss it like Europeans in movies did, but he held his hand out and shook her hand without squeezing hers too hard.

"Privet, I mean, hello. It is hard, yes, to speak this English? Too many words. Hello, hi, welcome, how are you… But, as American girl, let us talk this crazy English. Come, talk. Get to know each other, yes?"

Nodding, she was impressed with how polite, yet casual he was with her, speaking to her like a grownup. Going through two large doors, they entered a larger room lit by large lights with cables going from them to a box then to a camera on a tripod. They were on giant metal stands, and the shades on the lights were like opened umbrellas facing backwards. There was a rolling table with a MacBook, and two rolling chairs where he held out his hand for her to sit. She looked all around, and they were the only ones there. Without the overhead fluorescent lamps, the room felt and looked like pictures of photo studios she'd seen in movies and in magazines.

"I've never been in a photo studio. Those lights are so big!"

Laughing, he looked around, and shrugged.

"Nyet, no photo studio, hotel ballroom, just to take few pictures. Real studio, much bigger. High ceilings, lots of cables and paper and cloth backdrops. Places to put on makeup. For this, fine to use. So, have you been model?"

She was getting used to his way of talking. It was the same as how he'd say things in Russian, but he was using English words instead.

"No. This is the first time I've tried out for modeling. I'm not sure if I'm a model or not."

"Silly. No, it no work such way. It is photographer who does that. Here you are, beautiful girl, pretty face, such nice dress. How could you no look wonderful if I take picture what I see? Come, we get over that. I take picture, show you beautiful model."

Getting up, he waited for her to follow him to a spot the lights were pointing to. There was a long roll of gray paper going from the ceiling down to the floor, and it turned without a crease as it met the floor and kept going for about 10 feet. He pointed to a spot and tilted his head, letting her know to stand there. She did and was nervous, not knowing what to do.

"This is place for model. Stay here, listen to me, do what I ask, da? Good. No need for fancy stuff. Makeup is nice, dress nice, hair nice. You be nice, picture be beautiful. I go get camera, don't think about me, listen to me, do what I say. Good?"

Nodding, smiling, she watched as he picked up a large black camera and it had a cable attached to it going to a box on the floor, and a cable going from there to the computer. He went and adjusted two of the lights, stepping back to look, then tweaking them a bit, stepped back to be in front of her, but back in the dark, not where the lights were illuminating him.

"Good. Nice light, just right. I take many pictures, look at them after. Lights make pop, means picture taken. So, just stand, look to me…pop! There, first picture."

He went to the MacBook, and scrolled to where he took the first shot of her.

"Look perfect. Black dress shows curves nice, so now, we go."

Telling her to look down, eyes up, then turn her head a bit to the left or right, put her hands on her hips, turn around and look over her shoulder back his way, no smile, serious expression, pout a bit, mouth open a bit, head back, let hair fall behind, twirl around, make hair fly. After all that, he said to just stand sweet, be pretty, hands folded in front, and look like little fairy in forest, all shy-like. With each thing he asked, the lights popped, and it all happened fast. Finally, he came forward into the light.

"Look good, I sure… Very sure, maybe. Pull chair by computer, we look, see if I am good picture taker or not so good picture taker."

As she rolled her chair up to the computer screen, he rolled his up next to hers. Using the mouse, suddenly there she was on a large screen. She about gasped. She didn't know who it was. She looked like a famous model on a magazine cover. The gray paper was so different than it looked standing in front of it. It went from gray and faded to black, and it was a perfect complement to her black dress and her dark hair. As he clicked, each pose he had her do was amazing. Each picture had her looking different, and she looked stunning in each. The lights shaped her face in a way where she didn't see a 16-year-old girl. She looked 20, and she looked glamorous. Her skin tones were soft, the lights shaped her arms and legs, and her hair was so sharp she could see every strand. She couldn't believe how many different expressions she made. Each time he said to do something different, it caused her expression to change. The last image was the only one where she looked her age. Younger, she thought. With her hands crossed in front of her, head down, a shy expression, she was like he said, a little fairy in a garden.

She looked at him, and he smiled, nodding.

"I don't know… who is in pictures? Where is she? I want to sign her up, right now."

Both laughing, she agreed with him. She looked so different than how she did at home in her mirror. She understood he was a real photographer and had the fancy lights and camera. Even with all that, she could never have imagined she could look like off the cover of a magazine.

"How did you do that? I wouldn't ever guess that was me. Do you think they are good?"

Shaking his head, he started laughing.

"Please. Do no play innocent like you no know. God, he make you, not me. If you were no pretty, pictures no be beautiful. You natural. Made to be in camera lens. Each picture, perfect. I love them! You no know until pictures taken, but I had pretty good guess!"

She asked to see them again, and he went slower, pointing out poses that would be good for this or that. He clicked on a menu item, and she heard a soft noise. He got up, went to a printer against the wall and brought back a print of one of her favorite pictures.

"For you, show family, see if they like."

"Thank you. This is so fancy, this paper. I'm going to frame it. But, no family. Just my mom and me."

He looked sad, showing concern.

"That hard life. Me too. Just like you. She's still in Russia. Nice place I bought her. I miss her when I go places, but have to make money. So, you like, I like. I think you can make money. You want I should sign paper? I want to."

Nodding, she watched him sign her agreement, and he shook her hand after that.

"Now, go tell mom you have big future. You in front of camera, me in back. We make some money. While I here, we take real pictures. Get shots, we show people. Get you all set. Fixed up. My assistant, she set all up. Lots of outfits, maybe swimsuit, dresses, shorts. Everything. Work all day, ya?"

Smiling, she said that sounded exciting. As they went out to the reception room, she saw a young girl waiting. She was pretty, but it was hard to tell what she'd look like in pictures. She had learned how things didn't always look the way they were. Vlad handed Jamie the agreement and told her to set an all-day shoot with outfits for Friday. Giving Angie a copy of the agreement, she gave her a folder for the photo and the paperwork, saying she'd call to confirm what time they would be starting.

As she put the photo in the folder in front of Jamie, Jamie asked if she could see. As she looked, her eyes grew wide.

"Wow, Angie. You look stunning."

Riding the bus home, she kept looking at the photo print. She still didn't believe it was her. She imagined it having a logo of a famous magazine and next to her, lettering that said she was the hot new girl everyone wanted.

She would remember thinking how "everyone wanted her" would soon have a new meaning.

　　　　　　　　　　　　　　　

Chapter Seven
Service Rendered

Hoping to get home before Cindy was off escorting gentlemen, Angie made it just in time.

"Mom, you waited!"

Cindy had postponed a rendezvous with a regular as she wanted to be there when Angie got home and find out how it went. She could tell by the glow she wore things went well, and she thought, why not? Angie was very pretty and just what the flyer said they were looking for.

"Of course. I want to hear all about it. I can tell how excited you are that it must have turned out good. So, what happened?"

"Well, I can sum it all up with this!"

Handing her the folder, Cindy opened it and there was the photo of Angie. She gasped as she hadn't expected her to come home with anything, let alone a picture. She couldn't look away, and she stared at it, and tears started to flow.

"This is so beautiful… You… You are so beautiful. I don't think I've ever seen such a pretty picture. I can't believe it. That must have been some photographer. Angie, you know what? This? This here? This is how I see you when I close my eyes and think about you."

Crying more, she was worried about getting tears on the print, and moved it to a counter as she pulled some tissues from her jacket pocket.

"Mom, this is just one. The guy took like twenty of them, and each one is better than the one before it. They were all amazing.

And he just put me in front of the camera and kept telling to look this way and that, and in about five minutes it was all over, and we looked at them and I was in a state of shock. And mom, he wants me to work, and we signed an agreement so he can take a bunch of pictures and start showing them to clients and all. I mean, like this Friday, I'm going there for an all-day photo thing and he'll take all kinds of pictures and get me started!"

A bell went off in Cindy's head. The photo was amazing, but things seemed to be moving very fast. She had signed a contract and was going to get a whole day of photographing her. She needed to be sure about it all, asking her to sit down.

"I hope it's all going to work out and you're a big success. But, let's talk about everything so I know what you're getting into, okay?"

Some of her smile left Angie's face, but she understood she was new to dealing with people, and her mother wanted to be sure everything was done correctly. She told Angie to tell her everything that happened. She explained everything, including that the company was Russian, and so was Vlad. She also said she signed the agreement because she was told that dealing with a Russian company, the age when someone could sign an agreement was 16. Cindy had all kinds of concerns after hearing it all.

"Angie, the thing is that this isn't going on in Russia. It's going on here. The age of consent is 18. That doesn't sound right because you're in America, so the law here is what matters. And the contract has a lot of things that are pretty worrisome for me. I'm not trying to dampen your happiness. I'm not. So, maybe it would be good to slow things down a bit and find out if this is all okay."

"Mom, it's all set for Friday, and they won't be here too long so this is important. If I do that, he may find another girl. We need this. We need to get out of here…"

"I know, I know. See, it's when things go fast… when you are pressured that mistakes happen. If he thinks you're that special, he'll wait. I'm sure he'll understand. Angie, you're a minor. He has you sign a contract like that, and you're locked in to working with him only. And they're in some little motor hotel? Yes, he takes wonderful pictures, but the other things worry me. I want to make sure this is okay. Please, we are here for each other, and I'm going to be sure this is okay."

"Mom… I know you worry about me, but I want to do this. Please, I can tell if things aren't right."

Looking at Angie, Cindy knew she was swept up in the excitement, and it sounded like the photographer was a charmer. She knew all about charming men from that part of the world. She needed to be sure because he was from Russia. There are beautiful women there, and why is he looking in America? It may be a good reason, maybe not. She wanted to find out.

"Angie, I think I have a way to find out without calling and telling him to wait. My client tonight, well, he's a lawyer and I have known him for years. Single, I'm his only friend in a lot of ways. Well, he pays me to be a friend, but it's more than that now. I'd like to have him take a look at the agreement, and sweetie, he's from Russia, like all my clients are mostly. He'll know how to find out. Now, if he thinks things are okay, and I pray they are, then hooray! If not, better to find out now. Right?"

Sitting with her arms crossed, about to cry, Angie slowly nodded her head.

"Okay. It kind of makes me sad to make it all about lawyers and stuff. Does he know your illegal?"

"Of course, sweetie. That's why I only escort guys from the Ukraine or Russia. They understand, and they have their own problems. I've known him a long time, and he's always been nice. He offered to help me with getting citizenship, but I didn't tell him about the shootings and all, so he asks now and then, and I explain I'm not ready. I'll tell him everything you told me, and let's see what he says. Okay?"

Nodding, Angie went and hugged her. She knew her mom was protecting her. With all she had been through, she was careful, and she remembered she had her doubts earlier too.

Taking the folder, Cindy gave Angie a kiss goodbye, saying she wouldn't be long. Just the lawyer for about four hours, and maybe a bit longer as she hoped he would review the contract.

Walking down the street to a snack shop, it was where Yorgi always waited for her each week. She didn't want him to see she lived in a trailer park, and he respected she wanted to meet in front of the snack shop. His car was there, running. He drove a Mercedes and had done well helping immigrants but had never been successful with women. He worked all the time, was overweight and balding, not too good looking, and he wasn't much in bed. He paid her full rate plus a tip, and she always treated him special. Even though he was single, he had always preferred a hotel room as he lived in an apartment building and said his neighbors were far too curious and he preferred not to be asked private questions. None of that mattered to her. He paid well, was respectful, and he hadn't missed a Wednesday night in four years.

As she got in the car, she gave him a kiss and he asked how she was.

"Well, I have need of your help. I'd be happy to pay you for it, or make tonight a freebie. My daughter needs an agreement looked over, and you're the only one I can trust to tell us if it's okay. Would you be willing to take a bit of time to do that?"

Pulling away, he asked a few questions, and she gave him a good overview by the time they pulled into the Marriott Suites where he had a room booked far in advance for their meetings. As they walked into the room, he said he would be happy to look it over, and maybe look the firm up. Smiling and happy to hear it, she said she'd make it a freebie then. He shook his head.

"Don't be so provincial. Of course, pay I give you. It's just me reading. Do me nice like you always do while I read. You work, I work, I think I get better deal."

Laughing, she said it was a deal. Nodding, he sat in a stuffed arm chair as he watched her undress. Cindy was a slightly older version of her daughter. She was 28, and as an escort, looking sexy was how she made the most money. She was trim, had beautiful breasts that were popular with all her clients, long legs with lace-topped hose, and her face was youthful and pretty. She had become expert at comforting lonely men, and she gave them more than most girls would for the money. Most of all, she was beautiful, sweet, and had a great smile. As she pulled off her dress, under it she wore a lace bra and panties, each matching and black, and wore a garter belt for the lace hose. Pulling off the bra, she leaned over him and he licked and sucked her nipples as she started rubbing him through his pants to get him excited. After she pulled up and kissed him, she stood, pulled down her panties, then threw them onto the bed with the bra.

She knew he liked looking at her naked, but she left the garter and hose on as he liked that as well. She had her pubic hair trimmed to a small heart shape, but no hair on her labia. Turning around to show herself from behind, taking her hands she rubbed her cheeks and she heard his breathing deepen. Then, she bent over so he could see all of her fully. He was breathing and panting, saying she was such a beauty. She had kept her heels on, and that made her tall and extended her legs nicely. Standing up, she turned to him and saw he had the folder in his hand. She bent over and pulled down his pants and underwear, and he was erect. He seemed more excited than normal, and she guessed he was feeling important being needed by her — as she was needed by him. She started working on him, going slow to give him plenty of time to read the document. She wanted to be gentle so he could enjoy being taken care of, yet able to focus on the agreement.

Putting herself between his legs, she had put a pillow on the floor where she would be kneeling for quite a while. He opened the folder and began looking the items over, but she made sure to look up at him as he would look down at her now and then and loved seeing her eyes fixed on him.

He read the agreement several times over, and when he was done, he put the envelope down and said it would be good to finish him up as he wanted to make a call and didn't think he'd be able to talk normally while having sex. She knew he was about to climax as he put his hand on himself as she moved hers away, and he started stroking himself as she licked him with moans and sighs. That did the trick.

After licking him clean, she rested her head on his leg, still kneeling in front of him. He looked at her, and suggested they sit on the bed. He didn't want her kneeling like she was as he talked about things, and he was respectful that way. She remained naked, and he kept his pants off as they both got on the bed.

"Glad, I am. Good you show me. This, well, bad to sign, but still time as no work started. It be lie, this okay to sign at 16. No legal here. And is too vague. He can tell her to do more than take pictures or be in video. It may be porn video. And part, here, it says what clients want of her. That may be sex. No, not good. Russians like him, you deal with snakes. I make call, man who can go online, get on Russian database of bad men, look him up, look up company, see if is in his name. May be, may not be. I make call."

She laid with her head on his chest and could hear both sides of the call. It took a while, but she could hear that a man named Morozov was a known pimp and made porn movies. Nothing other than girls complaining he never paid them, and he disappeared one day. That was all he could find. After hanging up the phone, Cindy was grateful for all he had done and wanted to give him a wonderful thank you.

As he started to tell her what was said, she said she heard it all, climbed on top of him and knew all she would do would ease his worries… At least for that night.

Chapter Eight
Tonight's the Flight

"I was so worried she'd start talking to me in fuckin' Russian."

Jamie was sitting in the mock photo studio, looking at Jack. He was right about coming close to being revealed he wasn't "Vladimir."

"It can be fixed. We just let you speak American, no Russian. It does help explain why there'd be work in Russia, but we can explain that some other way. We have a nice bevy, and just Friday to do her shots so they see what they're buying. If she does, say no, you will only speak English in America."

"I did that, and it worked okay. Yeah, she's going to be worth the most, so I'll try to get her naked. At least in a thong. You set to be the stylist?"

Walking to a box, Jamie came back with a small triangle and three strings.

"Jack, all the twats hang their asses out on Instagram. Tell her where the money shoots are they go topless. You know the drill. I'll just hand it to her and tell her this is what we do. She doesn't know shit about real work, and we play like we do. Don't worry about it. Go fuck that Jenny. Get your mind off this stuff."

"That is the first good thing I've heard today. You fuck her up? How much you give her?"

"She's conscious, not knocked out. It's E. She's trippin' and smiling at the air. Put your cock in her mouth and she'll think it's a lollypop. Christ, she's 14, enjoy it. I have work to do. The keycard is on the table. 246, last room in case it gets loud."

Turning all the gear and computer off, Jack said he'd secure her, but she still needed to be knocked out.

"I left that in the minisafe. Don't mar her, okay? No bruises. Get your ass out of here."

Grabbing the keycard off the long table where Jamie worked, just holding it felt good. He had joined Jamie for money, but young ass had become more important than his cut. He recalled meeting Jamie at a porn shoot, and she was the producer. She found young runaways, drugged them up, and he filmed them doing all types of sick sex. They didn't even know what they were doing. The men in the shoots did, and they propped and positioned them, pulled their hair out of the way for his camera, and it was an assembly line operation. Same guys, endless girls. He talked to Jamie and said he'd like to do POV where they were sucking him off as he filmed from the guy's eye view. She had agreed to start each girl doing him first, and she learned he was a good actor. He wondered what happened to the girls after each shoot as they were in films one time, but never twice. She looked him over and knew he was hooked on getting pussy without working for it, and she told him to hang back after a shoot one day.

"Jack, enjoying those sweet assholes and mouths? You're doing, what, five or six a day?"

"Oh, yeah. I can't get enough. And you have them so fucked up. What are you giving them?

"Opioids and some coke. It works for a while. I'm glad you're having a good time, but I must say, you don't ask them enough questions. All I hear you ask is how much they love your cock. Ever ask them how old they are?"

Looking at Jamie, she was cold and serious. She was holding a folder and handed it to him.

"Yeah. Good to ask a thing or two. All that POV of you with your dick in their ass or mouth? Be just fine if they were street legal. Not one of them are over 16."

Rifling through pages of model sheets, there were their photos, ones of him with them, and copies of drivers permits. They were all underage. He realized she was going to use it on him.

"You're the producer. That's for you to weed out. I don't see them except naked, and they don't have purses or IDs when I do."

Taking the folder back, she smiled, looking into his eyes.

"True. But, remember, I didn't fuck them. You did. It's your dick up their ass. And I'm not a producer. I'm temp labor. Really, do you think I'm that stupid? No, it's you on the credits as producer. And what a bad thing to be using underage girls... Oh, these are just copies. Originals are tucked away. But take that scared look off your face. I think it's time for you to move up in the world."

Getting into the elevator, he recalled how clueless he had been. He wasn't clueless now. He shook from that night when she told him he was moving up in the world. She said it was time to learn why none of the girls appeared more than once.

"Those videos are sent live streamed to my clients. Most in Russia. By the time they fuck the last of the guys, I have prices for each one. They're up for bid. Highest bid thing. And, come with me, I'll show you what happens next."

Leading him to a large room with about twenty beds, there were curtains dividing them, and a large woman injecting one who was making noise. He realized they were all being kept drugged. He was shook up, but remembered she had set him up by his onscreen exploits with all of them, and proof they were all underage. He asked what the hell all of it was.

"Inventory. You'll learn all too soon. Tonight, we have a chartered plane to Russia and these girls will all be going to their owners. You and I, we're going too. Meet our most loyal buyers. They want to meet you."

He followed Jamie as she supervised the large woman taking each one to a large rental truck, and they were all laid in the back on padding, then the cargo door shut and locked. Next, a ride to a hangar where a jet waited, and after the huge hangar door was closed, the girls were tied, gagged and put on the plane, most all of them asleep. He was somehow sickened by it, but it excited him more than anything else. He had fucked each of them, and now it was someone else who'd be getting his seconds.

"Enjoy the ride. No fucking any on the way. They're clean and ready for inspection."

Sixteen hours later, they were in Russia. In the plane hangar, large men came in with pieces of paper stating which number girl their boss had purchased, and they took them out still drugged. In no time, the plane was empty. He asked how much she had made in total.

"An even million. About fifty a girl. These Russians have so much money they don't haggle. They'll make a hundred times what they paid for each one.

That was Jack's first run of trafficked girls. Jamie told him she wanted out of porn, and to get better ones through modeling auditions. She was right. The porn girls were not as valuable — or as young — as the want-to-be models. He agreed to be the photographer and he earned a 25% cut and it was piling up, all tax free. He forgot about what he was actually doing, and the girls were just product to be sold. It was as simple as that in his mind.

Putting the keycard in the door, a 14-year-old he had "tested" was floating around the room naked except for some silk flowers from a vase in her hair. She came up to him, stared in his eyes, and she was smiling and saying he had come to make her a little pony. He said he would like to go for a ride. Next, she was on all fours, crawling around him, saying she was ready to be mounted. Taking off his clothes, he knew he was in for quite a ride, and she was sweet and delicious. Not even a hundred pounds, he reached and flipped her upside down as she said "Oh, wow" over and over as he put his face deep into all her holes as she sucked on him, saying it was a big lollypop, her brown hair so long it cascaded down to the carpeting.

Each day was a new girl, and each was the same, but different. The way they sucked was never the same, the way they tasted was different and unique. The way they moved was what excited him most. Their walk, their crawl, the way they knelt, the way they came. The sounds they made, the sighs, the whimpers, and as the drugs wore off, the way they cried, the looks on their faces when he smacked them to shut them up, and the way their eyes popped when he covered their mouths to stop their screaming as he threatened to kill them if they didn't stop.

He could have given them more ecstasy or whatever Jamie had provided, but he got off on the awakening, the fear, choking them, threatening them, putting a washcloth in their mouths as they feared for their life as he fucked them and came from seeng their fear. It's when he felt most aroused and powerful. Sometimes he was so high from power, he put his cock hard down their throats to where they couldn't breathe, and they died from suffocation as he came. He knew Jamie would be pissed, and he told her to take their sale price out of his cut but it was an accident. He said he couldn't tell as they were so drugged. He had done that two times, and he wanted it to happen more as that was his ultimate way of getting off. The only thing that stopped him every night was he knew Jamie would pop a cap in his head as he was messing with the merchandise, and it cost her reputation for the sale. He told her he needed to get off by choking, and lied it wasn't to kill them.

 Innocence Taken

"You're one sick fuck, Jack. Really fucking sick. Want that shit? You couldn't go out and find ones on your own? You had to use mine?"

She had a 45 in her hand and it was pointed to his face. She would use it. He had seen her use it before, and she was ready to kill him at any time.

"So, what fucking luck. You're so good at the photographer shit, so charming, but you just have to be fucked up and get off by choking them? And two end up dead from that shit? Fuck, you are so pathetic. Do you know what a sick prick you are? Fuck… ah shit… You are going to fuck this all up. I'm going to end your shit right now…"

He sat, frozen as she started to squeeze the trigger. She didn't hesitate. He could only stare and his mind was empty. In a second he'd be dead. Then, he saw her finger stop. He thought how funny it was that he could see that slight release and nothing else. He then realized that was all that mattered. Her finger on the trigger was the same as his hands around a young girl's throat. He understood. He'd lay off if he wanted to scare them again, just get them choking then pull out and get off doing it.

"First off, thank me you fucker. I'm going to work this different."

He sat, not able to move, but managed to quietly say, "Thank you. How?"

She didn't pull the gun away, and she was still ready to fire.

"Do all the same shit, but no harming my merch. Once in Russia, that's where you go get yourself off. Pay for it. You make a lot. The fuckers I sell to have lots of ones they can't make more off of. Ask them what they want for them and choke away. Do that, I don't give a fuck if you do. But anything with what's mine, you're one dead fucker. I'll just off you. No more talks."

He agreed. They made flights every two weeks, and he was making so much money that paying for girls in Russia didn't matter to him. In some ways, it made him more excited as he could do even worse to them there. And he started to. Jamie had heard of some of the messes he made, and she told him there's always a line. It wouldn't be her offing him, it would be some Russian prick who'd gather up his pimps and they'd all watch. She told him it was his choice, and walked out.

Fucking the girl that night, he imagined her being one of the throw-aways he'd choose when they were in Russia the next night, and that got him off enough to cover her face in cum. She needed to be cleaned up, but he'd call Jamie first to inject her for the truck, and he'd wipe her clean. Jamie didn't care about the cum, but she did look for any bruising, checking the throat, pussy, asshole, then all over. He knew better than to make that mistake as she always had her gun, and she was always reminding him that he was a sick fucker and she could find so many guys as good as him.

"Jamie, I'm done. She's about down from the ecstasy, and I don't want to shut her up and bruise her. Ready to take her?"

The phone clicked from her hanging up. She was just a few doors away, and she had her own keycard. As she came in, he had a wet washcloth and a towel, and he was about done. Jamie pulled her legs and ass apart, then rolled her over looking for any signs of possible bruising. She spotted one yellow patch, then looked up at him.

"That's something she had already. Knees and girls this age. She'll be in a garter and hose. You fill her with cum?"

"Just down her throat. Nothing else. I fucked her, but was careful."

Pulling both her holes opened as far as she could, she needed to check. Nothing was oozing out and she couldn't see anything, so hearing the girl start to moan from the pain of her inspection, she

                                    Innocence Taken

told Jack to hold her down. Going into her purse, she had a vial and a syringe, carefully pulling some cocktail into the tube to a mark she had made with a Sharpie. Tapping it, she went to her feet and injected it between her toes where it wouldn't be seen. It always left a bruise anywhere else.

They both sat on the floor waiting as the girl eventually fell off into a coma-level sleep. They had to get her to the truck, and it was waiting in the basement garage near the elevator door. Getting the girl into a extra large black trash bag, they left the top loosely tied to allow air to enter. She told Jack to get the baggage cart outside the door. He opened the door, pulled it in, then closed the door. Putting the bag onto the flat bottom of the cart, she held the door open as he pushed the cart out and went to the elevator. She had closed the room and joined him. Once in the garage, they both lifted the bag into the rental truck. Jack drove to the hangar at the small airport, and it had a holding area for baggage. As they unlocked it, they carried the bag in, and after closing the door, they took her out of the bag and set her on the padding lining the floor. There were 18 girls all laying there, all asleep. She took out her syringe and went to each and juiced them up as she did each night until the flight was well on its way as they needed to be up, put in garters and hose, and fed. She had a different vial to keep them tame when they landed, and the plane put into a large private hangar used for the auction. Black curtains, music, a little stage to put them on display. It was well thought out, and her Russian partner owned the hangar and plane. He took a good cut, managed the buyers, and was a ruthless pimp.

"Okay, one more to go. Do all your shit as I need to send the photos before we go, but let's get it done early. As soon as it's dark, I want the fuck out of this shithole town. Are you going to off some bitch this time? Brian said he talked to you, and you fucking started to tell him he was asking too much. He has expenses you fucking idiot. He told me you do that again, you're dead. You really are fucking stupid. Think he's a man to haggle with?"

"He wanted to double the price!"

She stared at him, disgusted. She was losing her patience with him.

"Then pay it. That, or don't do any. Now, I want you to apologize to him, and say you're just a stupid fucking pervert. Then give him the money, and an extra payment to apologize. Not an advance. To show respect. Got it?"

"Yeah. You know he's just being a dick because he can."

Jamie sat, more pissed than ever at how stupid he was. He did the job, but he was pushing her limits. She'd needed to find a replacement.

"You motherfucking sick fucker. And some girl gets dead just because you can pay?"

She wanted to shoot him in the head right then. She had her hand in her purse, holding her gun. She sold girls, and that was risky enough. His killing shit was crossing the line. Too much exposure, and it gave her partner, Brian, one up on her. He'd probably taped each girl Jack offed, and she knew he'd use it at some time to punish her. It took all her resolve to not kill him right then. She decided to finish this run. The Angie girl would be the top dollar sell, and she knew that needed to happen first. After that, she'd pay Brian to off him. Then, she decided to just tell Brian she wanted to do it, and if he wanted to show his goons how she operated, gather them up. She'd say in exchange, no charge for disposal. If he didn't want the show, she'd pay him. Either way, it was his last run.

Getting back from the airport, Jack said he'd have things ready on time, but needed to sleep. She said she'd be pissed if he didn't have it all set up in time as she turned to go to her room.

She needed to talk to Brian before she got her sleep. She used an encrypted satellite phone for the call.

"Brian, no, no problems with the goods. I want to see if you wanted to put on a show for your new guys. No, not about pussy… about what happens when someone fucks up. I need to put a 45 in Jack's head… yeah, I know, you make money off him but killing girls? You'll make more whoring them out for chump change, really, and the risk is he'll do it here… I think you take a risk too. He knows too much, and he'd fuck you over if he had to… Okay, we agree. So, we have one more, the top dollar girl, then we head out tomorrow night. So, want to put on the show, or I'll just do him and pay you to put him through the chipper… Good. I'll pop him, and I think your guys will learn a lot seeing me do it. How did your clients like the last batch… Good. Yeah, the top girl is just 16, but after her I'm not taking any over 16 now… Younger? Well, that's what, down to 10? I can do it, but it will take a bit of time. Moms show up for those things, so I'll have to go slow at first… Oh, the 14 to 16s… Sure, no stopping those. It will cost more to get down to 10… Yes, I know you can get twice as much… Hey, I'm all for twice as much. Like I said, let me figure out how best to do it. It'll probably be grab and snatch shit, not fashion shows. Lots of risk. Do you have any guys who I could bring here for it, then bring them back each time… Yeah, I think that would be good. Well, let's use me doing Jack to show them what I'd do to them if they fuck up at all… Yeah, sounds good. Want to pick one for a trial run… You sure of him… Oh, he does it there? That's just what I need. Speak English… Excellent… Yeah, all set then. See you in what? 48 hours… Oh, these are all top dollar bitches. I did this shit town full of low life, and they'll probably see being owned as a step up… Yeah, all tall, thin, long hair. Flawless skin. Sweet ass, all top quality… Yeah, dinner with a new buyer? Sure… Oh, I see. He wants the tens… Okay, I'll ask him what color hair, body type, all that… No, you talk money, I'll talk cunt type. Sounds good. See you soon."

She'd need to think about the new request. With his guy, he knew how to do it, and she'd learn from him. She needed to keep the runway auditions going, so she'd need a new photographer. And he'd need to be okay taking pictures of the new merchandise.

She'd need to find one who got off on that. The world was one fucked up place. That shouldn't be hard to find. There were sites where guys sold pictures of those, so probably best to find one from there. They'd be sick, like Jack, but with ones that sick, they already knew what they wanted, and they knew the risk.

A few miles away, Angie was lying in bed, unable to sleep. In a short while, she knew her life was set to change. She was too excited to sleep. Her way out of Aurora had come. Soon, she'd be far away from the Hunter Motor Home Estates.

Chapter Nine
Taking a Flyer

"Mike, good job with that nab last night. We have his laptop and flash cards. Out in plain sight."

Sitting back in his tilting office chair, Mike nodded, knowing it was a righteous bust. Some go to plan, but the pervs were getting smarter each day. The internet had no way of restricting the dark web. Although referred to as the dark web, they were web sites like any other but like much online, they were cloaked and near impossible to locate who ran them, the servers they were on, or stop them.

Among the many dark web sites showcasing illegal or confidential information were one where officers and agents were identified with photos with home and office locations, and ways to hack into their accounts with screen names and email addresses. All such information for them sold using another untraceable tool, Bitcoin. The sites offered constant updates on where most stings were about to take place.

Knowing information once near impossible to get was now available for a price, he knew it would get worse. Part of his job was to be one step ahead of the dark web, and turn the tables on them by posing as a nefarious entity seeking such activity. He thought of them as stupid, arrogant fools. They did what they did because they thought they were smart. All lowlife, none of them more than self-taught hackers or working with scammers, they couldn't conceive that people like him existed. Ones who knew what they were, how they thought, how arrogant they were, and most of all how exposed they actually were. They were stupid men living stupid lives thinking they were so smart. He'd shake his head at how easy it was to take any of them down. The problem he faced was the sheer volume of them. The numbers grew each day, and for him it was about selecting ones doing the highest volume.

Go after the big data suppliers, then offer them some reduction of their sentence if they'd tell all the names of the ones they sold to. They always did. The same lack of morals that made them money selling illegal information made it easy for them to essentially sell-out their client list. It was the best way to go about it.

"Thanks. An easy take. Laying off them until they get overconfident works okay, but I've been meaning to talk to you about moving to direct takers. The online stuff? We have so many guys who can take my cases. That's in hand. I want to go after recruiters who are too smart to go online."

Standing with a cup of coffee from the office pot, James looked surprised. Mike was tops in playing the online traps and he hadn't mentioned wanting to do anything else. He asked why. Mike looked at him and was more serious then he'd ever seen him before.

"C'mon, James. I'm a field agent. I do that better than I do this. I want ones who aren't going after a single kid. I want the organized groups. They don't do anything online. I took this to see if they were moving online with it, but that's not happening. Dark web is for pervs. The rich clients? They call on encrypted lines, meet for dinner. Show up at auctions in private hangars. I want back in the field. I hate to say this, but if you don't move me, I'll quit. I'll do it without the agency."

James put down his cup, shocked at how certain the message was. He also knew Mike was someone who did exactly what he said. He would quit. His only question was why.

"Mike, okay. If you think the tech guys can take over what you've been doing, I'll go with that. I'll have to talk to the tactical group. See if they'll want you onboard. So, why now? What happened?"

Reaching into his satchel, Mike pulled out a newspaper and handed it to James, then reached in and pulled out a flyer and handed it to him as well. He said he'd explain what was there.

"This. Okay, the flyer. Looks the same as ones you see all over the place. Come-ons for making money for family portrait photo packages. But large traffickers learned they could play that angle. The lure of fame and fortune has a strong appeal. The girls' show up for an audition, they drug them, take them, then in a day or two, they're being sold overseas. I've been tracking some small players online, but these… they're different. The legitimate studios, yeah, they're ripoffs but are legit businesses. They have studios, stay in one place. Business license and all. Look at this one. In town for a few days, then gone. They move on and use a new name. Same pitch, girls show up, they grab and go. Then when parents realize their girls haven't come home, no trace. And, at those ages, girls do run away so police say wait 24 hours, they ran away and will come back. These auditions? Any hotel near an airport with a meeting room is their location, three four days most. I found this one. Active this week. Runaway Elite. They fucking come right out and say it's for runaways. Dreamers too. Young girls all want to be models. So, that's part one. Read it through."

James looked it over, reading it over shaking his head at the verbiage, then nodded.

"What arrogance. They're basically saying what they're doing. This part… we can't wait to have you… real subtle. I get it. So, find the drifters, What's the second part? This newspaper?"

"It's what pushed me over the edge. Page 12, the article about the girl and her mom. Read it, you'll get it."

Girl and Mother Missing

Local attorney Yorgi Alexander has reported his client, Cindy Wilson, aged 28, and her daughter, Angie Wilson, aged 16, are missing and is asking anyone who has seen them or had contact with them to call him or the local police. He stated that his client, Cindy Wilson, told him her daughter headed to a model audition with Runaway Elite, a runway model agency, on Friday, April 18th. He added that when attempting to contact Cindy Wilson, she did not answer his calls or messages, and visits to her home were made but she has not been seen. After 24 hours, he reported them missing to the local police. Filing a report that the two have not been found or heard from, he worries that the daughter may have been abducted, and that in searching for her daughter, the mother may have been abducted as well. If you see anyone matching the pictures shown here, please contact us, Mr. Alexander, or the Aurora police.

James looked at the pictures. One was of the girl, a perfect studio portrait of her in a simple black dress. The other was of the mother, a more-than-attractive woman, also posed in a studio shot, but in revealing attire. Closing the paper, he handed it, and the flyer, back to Mike.

"That's pretty clear. Girl goes to audition, snatched, taken out of the states, mother goes to find her, either murdered or, from her looks, trafficked too. So, find out anything more about the Runaway group?"

Putting the paper and flyer back into his satchel, he nodded. He was calm and confident as he always was, leaning back.

"Oh, yeah… I traced them. Not easy to track as they don't put ads in the paper. Just flyers in stores and other easy spots like tacked to a light pole. So, I figured they worked a general area. One state at a time, or working towns around a major city. I went into small town police records and found filings for missing girls aged 14 to 16. All in crappy towns where drugs and murders are priority, not missing kids. It was easy to see their tracks. All had missing girls in that age range, and the actual reports said the girls had gone off to an audition. Some had names of the audition. Most were plays off the Runaway name. Just changed enough to make direct searches hard for local police to do search like we can do. This one stood out because of the mother and the lawyer. He raised enough noise to get in the local paper. Man, it's so clear. They don't even need to hide. Nobody cares. I do, though. Now it's just the who, and where do they take them to? I wan't to bust them."

"Hold on, I'm going to call Henry in tactical, see if he's been on them."

"James, I can answer that. They really aren't on this at all. Call him. I already did. He was mildly interested, saying they had a heavy caseload and all that bullshit. I don't know. He should have jumped on it, but he didn't. I'm not sure that will work. If they put me on some stupid large sting nonsense, I don't know what I'd do. Maybe I should just resign."

Staring at him, James understood his concern. He said if he could hold out a few hours, he'd see if there was some way to tackle things differently. James was a top official who knew the limits of how agencies worked. If anyone could make changes, James would be the one who could. He said of course, but not much longer. James nodded, saying he would rattle a few cages.

Working with a few new agents through lunch, he was confident they understood his tactics. He noticed James walk in, waving him to come to his office.

"Close the door. Okay, I think you can work with this. I bypassed tactical. They have a lot going on and a limited mission profile. I went right to Alan, the bureau chief… you've met him… and laid out what you showed me and what you want to do. Of course, he instantly said small time stuff, not even for future exploration. That's when I told him you'd go rogue and go it alone. He knows enough about you because when you came onboard, I told him. You going it alone — but knowing what we do, well, that stopped that bullshit. He asked what the fuck I suggest. That's what I hoped to hear. I told him you work the field and report it to me. I'll tie it into our mission somehow. He said he wan't hot on you going it alone and asked who'd back you up, and I just stared at him…"

Mike laughed, then James joined in.

"Mike, it was just us sitting there, staring each other down. Finally, he said okay, you're your own backup. It worried him as how would he know what you were doing. I said a thing called a report. Rather than duke it out all day he green-lighted you going field, and report weekly or as needed — nothing left out. If it goes like you think, he even said more field agents could be approved. So, sound good? I mean, geez, you still have a paycheck and even worse, have to keep reporting to me…"

Again, they both laughed, and Mike picked up a baseball that James had on a stand on his desk. He had pitched in college, and was proud of it.

"James, thank you. He wouldn't have listened to me as he's by the book, but you played ball, so you knew the right pitch."

Happy to tell him the news, as Mike would be reporting to him he decided it would be a good time for setting up a way to keep informed and learn where he'd start. He wasn't worried as Mike had started as a field agent and had extensive training in firearms and self-defense, but knew he must have a starting point due to the newspaper article.

"Mike, I can see you're determined. You said the newspaper article was the breaking point. You did your searching and I'm sure you have a plan. We need to setup some protocol for you to report. I want to know you're safe, but also where you are in case you need help. There's no backup lined up, so out there on your own, I'm your lifeline. So, you showed me the article. That who you're going after first?"

"Of course, or I wouldn't have shown you. Now that you've done your magic in this maze, I'll tell you why I put it as an imperative. I have another page to show you."

Pulling a folded sheet from his hip pocket, Mike handed it to James who carefully unfolded it. He read it, then looked at Mike, not sure of what he was planning.

"That is my ticket into that ring. As you see, it's a posting on a dark site seeking a photographer to do what they term school portraits. That's code for really young children. It also says they want a person who loves their work, and that's code for a ped, and then must be willing to travel at a moment's notice. Not really a code, but I read it as being part of delivering or transporting children. It's clear that it's grade school level as it says grammar school experience a must…"

"And you, Mike, before signing up, were a glamour photographer. Solid. I get it. So, two questions. First, I imagine they'd want to see your work, and I mean the type they want. Second, how do you know it's the same group?"

"The files on my PC? How many evidence shots from pervs of kids that age? I'll need your okay, but I'd grab about 100. Those are really bad, and I'd take the worst. Ones that have never been distributed as we seized them from camera cards. I'll inventory them in and out. It's them, I'm sure. They have a pattern of naming, and this is from one they use for gear and renting trucks. Morozov LLC. The ad, it's from that name. It has to be them. I have more than required, and I won't reply online from here. I'll buy a burner phone and text them a few cropped samples. I'm sure they'll call first, then a meetup. I'll go packing, and won't hide it. I have my dark web identity and they can find me out on the prowl online. I think that's all they'll need. I just need you to activate my identity and cut it loose from here completely. They may be able to track it as I think it's a Russian group, and they can hack like hell."

"What makes you think it's Russian?"

"Easy. Morozov. Russian name. I checked, they have a US LLC under it, and a Russian corporation with the same name. I haven't gone deeper, but one of our guys can trace finances and transfers. The US LLC is flat out smart. It's category is fashion photography. So, I leave here, go to Walmart for a phone, use one of our proxy credit cards, and see if I get a call. If you approve, I'll download the image files to a safe cloud, the one I use, VPN it all, which they'll expect. That's my plan. Sign off on the pics and use of assets, and I'll report as needed, but always at least once every week. I'll use your safe email, no calls here. I'll email you my number. You know all the protocols, so I'll stick to it all. So, is it a go?"

"As if I have a say so or choice. Yes, if it were anyone else, I'd be worried. Here… go get confiscated firearms… their serial numbers are all burnt off, so take your pick. I put three on here. I'll let them know and just sign for them. Well, this is all so fast, I wish I knew more. But we won't do any tracing or set off any alarms. If it is flat-out get them now, I'd feel better, but I can only guess you're going after the ties in Russia."

Nodding, Mike said he was going to gather all the places, people and sources before doing anything. When he calls, it will be for all of it. James just shrugged, saying that with a rabid dog, cutting off one leg just pisses him off, so he understood.

Leaving loaded with files, firepower, and all his alternate identity documents, he only had to get a phone, then he'd be in touch with them. He kept seeing the pictures of the two in the paper. Having a specific objective focused him. He would find a way to get in, then say he saw the article and got off on doing both the mom and daughter. It would be an advance against future earnings.

Chapter Ten
Fresh from the Back

Neither Jack nor Jamie expected Angie to show up with her mother. As they entered the room, they hid their expressions, but had a chance to look at each other. Jack moved his eyes to the photo room, and Jamie said for the two to sit and relax as they got everything set up and she picked out some special outfits.

"Jamie, you can tell her I do better with no one looking or telling her daughter what to do. That, or maybe send them both packing…"

Thinking, Jamie had dealt with such unexpected situations, and they would have the mother sit in and never make a move beyond that. She had already sent the first shots of Angie and there was already a buyer. They left that night, so she was in a bad place. She thought a bit more about it, then had an idea.

"Jack, we're going to turn this into some extra cash. Did you see the fucking mom? She's marketable. I never wanted to deal with of-age women as they don't fall for the audition shit, but I think we do her, and bring her with. Shit, that's a mother-daughter act. We can get a lot for that. Yeah, let's do that. When you go back out, do the number of how you have to take them together, they are a dream come true. All that. Get me some good shots of her alone, then the two together. Once I see them on my laptop, I'll send them off. If I get a nice price, I'll come in with the drinks and then we pack them up and get out of here."

Smiling, Jack said it was not what they normally did, but no problem. He added he wanted to fuck them both. Jamie shook her head, saying no, once on the plane, no messing with the goods. He shrugged, saying he was disappointed, but he'd be happy with some extra cash. Smiling, knowing that wasn't going to be how things worked out, she said she'd try to get them both in bathings suits at least. Laughing, he said that would be no problem as she was doing the wardrobe suggestions. He'd get them revved up, she needed to say what to wear. Looking at each other, they both nodded, and it was time to get them started.

"Angie, no... I can no believe you bring sister! It be like twins!"

Both Angie and Cindy blushed, looking at each other. Cindy had taken Yorgi's advice and accompanied her to the photo shoot. He had her worried and he suggested not raising any alarms, and that her showing up would prevent them from doing anything to her daughter. Early in the morning, as Angie got up after a sleepless night, Cindy was up, waiting, putting on makeup and telling her she was so excited she wanted to go with. Angie hugged her, saying that would be wonderful, and it was such a surprise. As Angie put on her new dress, Cindy found a conservative sleeveless dress, and with little makeup, low heels, and her hair worn back in a ponytail. She looked very much the suburban mother, though stunning and beautiful still. She didn't let on that she was worried based on what Yorgi had told her, and she acted happy all the way there on the bus.

"Hi, Vlad. I agree, we look so alike, but this is my mother! Cindy, this is Vlad. Vlad, this is Cindy."

Putting out her hand, Vlad took it and shook it, keeping his gaze on her, smiling. He stepped back, put his two hands together forming a mock frame like they did when making movies to block the shot. He shook his head, moving a bit from side to side to look Cindy over.

"Cindy, stunner. Stunner, you are. Please. Please to let me take pictures of you too. Then, if two beauties could be kind, take pictures of you together. I insist. It is too much to not capture what I see. Will you keep me from a life without such gift?"

Even with her worries, she saw the excitement on Angie's face, and it would allow her to be in the photo shoot to keep an eye on things. She acted embarrassed, but looked at Angie, nodded, then back to Vlad.

"Well, I think it would be a nice keepsake to have a pretty picture of us together. Okay! Why not? So, yes."

"My heart, it thanks you. Please, to come with me. Jamie, she will help with makeup, as if you need any! Well, that, and she has beautiful outfits. She is expert at what clients like, so she help you get best pictures to show world. Come, this way. Jamie, please, to help us start?"

Everything was set up to start taking pictures, and Vlad told them he would dazzle them with a simple shot standing with each other, then show them what beauty was. Doing a simple, classic pose, he fired off the strobe light, then called them to see it on the MacBook on the side table. It was a good picture, and they both stared at it. He had lit it where they had deep shadows, with their hair lit from behind. It was a classic magazine cover shot. Watching them look at it, them smile at each other, he knew it would be easy to get things moving fast and get them into some skimpy string bikinis.

Next, he took some classic portrait shots of Cindy's face, thanking her.

Walking up to them, Jamie said to follow her. She went to a rolling clothes bar, and it was standing by a dressing screen that was just a drape hung over a backdrop stand.

"Here's what I think will really sell. Angie, your dress is perfect, so Vlad will take some of you in that. Then, for both of you, these are so nice. Simple halter tops and perfect summer shorts to show your legs nicely. Flip-flops instead of heels. Then, I thought we'd go with the figure shot, first Angie, then you two together as that will be stunning. So, matching white go-where-none-dare bikinis.

That's what's in fashion right now, so we go with those. Angie, your makeup is just right. While you're doing your dress shots, I'll do a bit with your mom's hair and a bit of perfecting her makeup. Just go, Vlad's waiting."

Cindy was looking over to the lights popping, and then looked at the clothing that Jamie had picked out. She thought the halter tops and shorts were just a bit revealing, but was concerned over the bikinis. She looked at Jamie and held one of the bikini bottoms up.

"This isn't going to cover up much. I don't know…"

"Cindy, have you seen what's in fashion right now? Oh my God. They are wearing micro thongs and little triangles on top! That's the rage. I have those, but I think these are rather tame. Vlad knows how to shoot where nothing is too suggestive. Especially as it's a mother and daughter. Are you shy about wearing a bikini? You are so shapely, I know you'll look amazing. We have a policy. If we take pictures and you're not proud of them, we don't use them. I think this will be the shot that gets Angie lots of work…"

Putting the bikini bottom back down, she didn't want to create conflict, and she knew all too well what was in style, and the white bikinis were near as bad as the micro thongs. She had a great body, and she was more concerned for Angie as she hadn't been in a bathing suit since she was little. She also knew that Angie was sold on trusting Vlad and Jamie for her test shots, so she shrugged, saying okay, but she would ask to delete them if they were too suggestive.

"Spoken like a responsible parent. Hooray for you! Well, we'll try. Maybe you'll love them. Well, here comes Angie. I see you're all smiles so that must have been fun. Oh, let's decide on this now. Your mom was worried that the bikinis were a bit tiny. I told her they were the style clients want to see as that's what they're selling, and if you two don't like exposing that much, we won't use the shots. So, I've found in such instance to get that worry out of the way. I'll tell Vlad we can do the bikini shot first if you want to give it a try. There's the dressing area. I'll go tell Vlad…"

Without waiting to see if they agreed, Jamie walked away and went to Vlad. Angie looked at Cindy to see what she thought. Against her instincts, she learned how the girls were pressured and why so many did things they would not normally do. She just wanted to get through the shoot, then get out of there.

"It's not in good taste as it will show everything. You know I'm filled out and this won't hide much. But, I told her if we aren't okay, I'd say no. We'd both say no, I mean. I trust you to do right. So, hold your breath and lets put these damn things on."

Behind the screen, Cindy helped Angie get naked, then helped her put the suit on, tying the strings, then stepping back to look, telling her to turn around. The top was too little even as Angie didn't have full breasts yet. She was more upset as there was no back to the bottom. It was just a string going up and her cheeks were fully exposed. She thought about it, and decided that she would tell Vlad nothing showing her from behind. If he didn't agree, they'd change out of them. After that, she took off all her clothes and put the other bikini on. There was a standing mirror behind them, and she looked at herself. The top just about covered her nipples and her breasts were fully visible on the sides and bottom. The lower piece just covered her mound, and she already knew her bottom was fully on display. She shook her head, then looked to Angie.

"See, this is way too revealing. I'm a grown woman, and this sure shows it. I don't know. I'm really uncomfortable having you on display. Tell me. Look at me. Do you think this is right?"

Looking at her mom, then herself in the mirror, she turned around to look at her bare bottom fully shown. She turned to Cindy.

"Mom, you're right. I think a suit that doesn't have us naked would be okay, maybe. But, no. I don't want to even go out and tell Jamie. Let's change back, then do it."

Proud of Angie, Cindy smiled, then gave her a kiss on the cheek, saying she was proud of her.

Sitting in front of the MacBook, Vlad behind Jamie, they smiled at each other. It didn't matter if Vlad took pictures of them in the suits. Vlad had placed a micro 4K wireless camera to have a full view of the dressing area behind the drape. They had all the pictures they needed, including each of them naked. As They watched, Vlad said he'd hide the file, and Jamie went back to picking out clothes just in time. Angie came out in her dress, holding the suit.

"I'm sorry to be a stick in the mud, but neither of us felt okay in these. They show way too much. Can we just move on to the shorts and tank top? I hope those don't show too much either."

"Angie, that's why we have you try them on before anything. If you aren't okay, that will show in the pictures. And, I understand. The world today… way crazy, all the girls with their bums on display. Not even attractive. Here, I think these are just the right size. Your mom and you are both 0, and she'll sure fill this top out, and if needed, I have a 2 she can swap it for. Well, here… take the 2 top and see what is best. Hey, I'm going to go get some iced tea for us all. Do you both like it sweet, or plain?"

Sitting in shorts and halter tops, both agreed they looked good, and in the size 2 top, her mother looked just right. They sat with Vlad and Jamie and drank iced tea, and Vlad said the summer lighting setup for the swim wear was the same for the shorts and tank tops, so take it easy, and he was glad they had said they weren't comfortable in the revealing bikinis.

"Some girls, they live to show off body. Other girls, put value on body, no show off. What you no can see is best. Creates interest. You wonder what is under things. That is art of fashion. Right now, you look pretty. In bikini like those, nobody see that, they see everything else but pretty. Those faces. So beautiful. We make money with you with no bikini on at all!"

Jamie almost spit out her tea. She knew exactly what Jack was saying as not too much longer they'd be naked, no bikini at all as they were auctioned off to some oligarch. She looked over at him and he could see her smile as she took a small sip of undrugged tea.

"Ladies, okay, we have summer drink, we are all pretty and ready for fun outdoors. Finish up, and when you be done, we take nice pictures of the two beauties everyone will do anything to have!"

Holding up his glass of iced tea in a mock toast, they all joined in, Cindy relieved the session was almost over as no other outfits had been suggested. She was already getting tired as she hadn't slept before, and she wanted to take a nap, but shook herself to snap out of it. She saw Angie slumping in her chair, and as she reached out to wake her, her glass went flying and then all went dark.

Leaning over them, shaking them, Jack looked up at Jamie.

"Out like a light. We have so much time without the bikini shot. Oh, hell, let me fuck them. I'll come on them, not in them."

Not wanting him to get suspicious of what would happen later, she had never denied him such a request when there was time. She didn't see any harm if he came on them, and he was good about that when the goods were headed out. She nodded at him.

"Okay, I'm going to go take the signs down and get things all packed up. Fuck away. I don't know what good it is if they're not awake. I'll be back to make sure you don't fuck them up."

Getting out of his pants, he put his cock up Cindy's pussy after slobbering it with spit. He had pulled their clothes off, and had Angies' ass positioned to where he could lick it and stick his tongue up it as he fucked away on Cindy.

Jamie came in, pulled a chair over, pulled off her panties and pulled her dress up. Watching him, she started rubbing herself. He was exciting to watch, and she enjoyed seeing him fucking as it always got her off.

Soon, he pulled out of Cindy and started fucking Angie's ass with her on her side, Cindy positioned where he could lick her pussy and ass. Neither of the two moved except for his thrusts, and as he licked Cindy's pussy, he pulled away and looked at Jamie who was rubbing more spit on her clit.

"See the little asshole I'm fucking. She came right out of this cunt. Right out of this beautiful fucking cunt…"

He pushed his face into Cindy's pussy and stuck his tongue up her, sucking for air. Jamie watched and came as he said Angie came out of that glorious cunt.

Chapter Eleven
Love for Sale

Angie could only feel a vibration. She heard a rumbling sound as she was being jolted, then a screeching noise. She couldn't see anything although her eyes were open. She was in a dream or maybe awake but not awake and where was the iced tea she was drinking and why wasn't she able to move her hands or feet?

The screech changed to a rumbling noise again, and she felt herself moving forward but held back. She was drinking iced tea and looking at her mom and now she was hearing noises and being pulled and bounced around. She winced as she felt a bee sting her foot. The noise grew quiet, and she called out to her mom to see if she had fainted and had she ruined her pretty dress. She called but couldn't hear her voice and her mother wasn't answering and then she felt like she was floating… drifting up… maybe she was…

"She's out. I've been pretty shy with the dose, but I think the rest won't need anymore. I'm keeping her where she'll show how freaked she is when we put her up. They love to see them fucking scared."

For a private jet, it was large enough to lay twenty behind the four swivel seats up front. The other seats had been removed and the area was lined with thick foam to keep the girls from bruising. All drugged, they wouldn't rouse until they landed in Russia. Jamie had learned to dose them just enough to be able to stand up in the spotlight stage surrounded by curtains in a private hangar. She'd juice them with some amphetamine, put them in some nylons, and they'd be led out one-by-one for bid. Nothing about their bodies was hidden. The men who came would sit around the stage and just call out how much, and she'd keep tally on her iPad. The men had guards and vans without windows, and what happened to the girls after they wired their money was up to them.

For this trip, half of the more average ones were already bought by a trafficker who didn't care much about looks, just the lowest price. The rest were ones she put a starting price on that was fair, but often went ridiculously high if the man wanted the girl for himself, or for a client who had seen her picture and wasn't concerned about price. Once all the girls were sold, it was back on the jet and headed home for more. Business was growing with each trip, and the traffickers were wanting younger girls along with the teens. She assured them she would respond to their requests. She knew that added risk, but the money made it worth taking.

This trip had an added event, and the traffickers had been invited to watch how serious she dealt with privacy and how their purchases were treated. Jack was on his last run, and she decided to make it an added attraction. One of the traffickers had to be told a girl he had already paid for wasn't available. Jack had choked her. Jack had crossed the line, and she needed to show her buyer what she did with any man who ruined a deal. She had offered him a replacement that he agreed to and told him of her plans. He said he would enjoy watching a fool who messed with his goods get his reward.

As they landed and taxied, she began injecting the girls with a small amount of speed. They would be up, able to be shown but still in a fog. All she wanted was for them to be able to stand up, walk, and if they went into a panic, that was part of the show. They'd be naked wearing stay-up black nylons, and she had one pair of heels she'd use for the one on stage. The added leg was a must.

As the plane stopped, she heard the large hangar doors close and the jet's door opened. She was greeted by two large bald-headed men who would take each girl off the plane and gently guide them to the staging area where they had set up comfortable chairs for bidders.

Putting nylons on the girls, she watched Jack eying their pussies, thinking how that would be his last chance for such looks — and to kill girls. She sold women but harming or killing them was never okay with her. She knew it wasn't apparent, but she had a line that stopped at physically harming any girl. Killing them for sexual pleasure was something she understood happened, but she thought such men should be killed for doing so. Jack needed to be killed for taking their lives, not because it cost her money. She wanted the bidders and buyers all see what happened to a man who killed girls for sick pleasure.

After they were all ready, Jamie walked to the stage, greeted all her buyers, saying she offered a good selection, then asked that they please stay for a special message after the last showing. Watching the men nod, she escorted each girl up, turned them around, had them bend over, and invited closer inspection if desired.

The bidding went better than expected and for the climax of the sale, she brought up Angie. They all applauded, but she held up her hand saying that she had more. Jack brought Cindy to the stage, and putting her next to Angie, Jamie said they were mother and daughter, sold as a set, one price for both. The men stood up, all clapping and saying that it was delightful. They all walked up to them and looked them over. Close inspections took time, so both Angie and Cindy were waking enough to start showing fear, their eyes wide, trying to cover their breasts as the men rubbed at them, pulled their asses open, laughed at their surprise, and each started making offers that surprised Jamie as they were so high.

"Angie… what… where are we? What is this?"

Cindy just stared into her eyes, knowing that it was bad. She realized they had been drugged and they were in a nightmare. Everyone was speaking Russian, and speaking Ukrainian she understood all they said, knowing they were being sold. She was alert enough to know not to do anything to fight them.

"Just stay still. They'll hurt us if we fight…"

Standing, cold, naked, shivering, Angie was able to nod as she looked at Cindy, tears pouring out of her eyes, having a look so tortured yet trying not to provoke their captors. Cindy found herself more concerned about what Jamie was saying to the Russian man who had bought them than her own terror of what was happening.

"Brian, no, I don't have papers to prove it, but look at them. How else could they look the same? They aren't sisters, and I'm not an idiot or trying to fool you. When they're fully awake, you'll hear them talking. They'll prove it that way."

"Jamie, I no doubt you. No, never. But, Arabs, they no trust even me. Think you could maybe find something? They have bags with them. Purses? Must be something, da?"

"Will it get you more money?"

"Jamie, sweetheart. It get Brian more alive!"

She closed her eyes, and thought about it. She had a few ideas.

"Da. I shred all they brought. Nothing left to find. But I saw an article in their local newspaper about how they are missing. It has their pictures and how they were last seen by their lawyer. He's a Ruskie, but not a friend. He has an office. He must have things about them. It's a big risk, especially right now."

"Oh, you have answer, so simple. Get copy of paper. Or link to article, you know, online if there. That be more than I need. Other things? Can be forged. Newspaper? Lawyer? Perfect! This paper, you can get me?"

Smiling, Jamie felt relief, saying she would when she got back, and not to worry. She asked him if they were going out to his client as she could fix them up a bit.

"Nyet, no need. Client, he big politico. At world leader conference. I thought he may want them to give a little, well, what you call, incentive… to some leaders, but no, I think this for him. So, maybe week, maybe two, he comes for them. I have housekeeper take them, make them way he likes. Thank you for kind offer. So, show, is no over, da?"

"Once these two are in your limo, yes, a show. Have your men watch. It's a show of force."

Smiling, patting her on her shoulder, he told her to have a good time.

Hearing the man's plans, Cindy felt there may be a chance to get away. If they were being held for some man for a few weeks, anything was possible. She couldn't tell Angie yet, even in English, but it was at least a hope she could hold onto, for the moment.

A long Mercedes with completely black windows rolled up, and a woman got out of the back, a large, stern man holding the door open. The woman came, looked Angie and Cindy over carefully, then Jamie told them to be smart, not put up a fight, and go with the woman. They weren't shoved or pulled, and they were still in a state of terror but ended up in the back of the long car, it not moving. Cindy, near the window, could still see the little stage, and she was staring at it.

She watched Jamie stand on it and was talking to the men who had bid on the captives, and she noticed she was making some sort of speech, her hands up in the air, and she was getting nods from the men, now more than during the bidding as they had their guards and others there as well. She watched as two large men pulled Vladimir up to the stage, and he was fighting each step of the way. They put him behind Jamie, and she noticed all the viewers were in front of her, the only one behind her was Vlad.

She watched as Jamie pulled out a large silver gun from her bag, turned, and shot Vlad point-blank in the head as the two men stood holding him on each side.

Not wanting to alarm or frighten Angie more than she already was, she quickly turned her head to her, and pulled to hug her. She had seen how the world they were in dealt with problems. She did not intend to end up like Vlad, though thinking how glad she was he was dead. He deserved it. They all did.

Chapter Twelve
Model Agent

Mike went to his small apartment packing three Glocks, his satchel bulging with ammo that he had tried at the firing range, but never in real shootouts. Taking the guns out, he held each one to get the feel. They were right for his hands, and they had the precision tooling of a dependable weapon. Next, he looked at the assortment of ammo. He looked at the round nose bullets, knowing they had excellent range. Then, he looked at the hollow points which did the maximum damage to human tissue as they exploded on impact and were most always deadly. Two of the pistols were large, but one was small enough to wear in the back of his pants or even a jacket pocket. He loaded that one with round nose bullets and decided he'd start carrying it whenever he was out.

Having bought a pay-as-you-go phone, it was simple and easy to activate using a credit card that was part of a false identity for field agents. After that, he created a VPN on a Chromebook that was new and unregistered, and he decided to contact the person looking for a kiddie photographer. He loaded his pictures onto the Chromebook and put a few on his phone. After finding the want ad on a dark web site for peds, he simply said he loved such work — loved it as it was personally gratifying. Then, a few photos that just were innocent enough while being fully suggestive of what pictures would follow. He added he'd love to travel where real freedom and opportunities were, and he was available now.

He was sure it was Morozov LLC, and they were not that hard to track with the right access, which he had from the agency. Knowing no groups could hide if they were out recruiting in public, they had left a trail of recruiting followed by missing children reports. He didn't wish to contact any of the families or make himself noticed by anyone but needed to explain why he suddenly appeared out of the blue in the market. Thinking it through, he first thought of gaining a prison record, but that was so obvious, and worse, it could be checked if they knew any inmates. He decided to simply say he was working for another organization, but the head of the ring had been killed by an enraged father and it had fallen apart. There were so many small groups out trafficking, he knew they were allied with Russia so he made his background all about trade to African groups, where few dared go deep into that world and survive. It would give him status.

Finally, he pulled out a few of his old unpublished glamour shots that would show his prior life doing model portfolios. He still took pictures as an escape, and he was skilled at location or studio shots. He had plenty to make himself a good find for the group. He just needed to wait for an email or call.

It didn't take long. That night he was texted that if he would like to meet, some sweet treats at a nearby coffee house would be nice. He texted back saying if they had his favorites, he would be there. A Google map link came back, and it was a local bakery turned coffee house. Replying, he said he'd be there, and he'd be picking up some photo gear nearby so a perfect location. That said. he'd be easily identified as he'd have a pro camera and a tripod.

Versed in the code language that said things without saying anything that most would recognize, he was sure the meeting would be a go. He'd wear a leather jacket, look stylish but not too attention-getting. The jacket would hide the Glock, and he wasn't going to record anything or play games. He would treat things as if he were a total pervert and would love to be part of a group that supplied a steady stream to match his sick needs. He knew the language, and now he wanted to go deep and find how deep into Russia it all led.

Getting up early, he made sure he had no agency cards or items that could give him away. He changed his hair to look the role of a pervert who could behave himself when in public. Grabbing his

Lumix Full Frame, he carried it and had a carbon fiber tripod with a strap hanging over his shoulder.

Arriving ten minutes early, he knew whoever he was meeting would be there before him to check him over. Walking in, he went and ordered a danish with cherry filling in the middle and a latte, then looked around for a table. He saw a woman waving at him, and she was smiling like they were old friends. She was about thirty, attractive but conservatively dressed. She had a canvas briefcase and was drinking an iced tea. He waved back, got his roll and latte then went to the table, acting as she had, glad to see her.

"Nice touch. Ordering a sweet thing. I know you like them. Not my taste, they're so pricey."

He knew she was giving him all the code words, and he nodded.

"Oh, I know. Especially when there's not enough of them. They are so popular. I'm surprised to find some here. Good choice. Nice spot."

She laughed, and they each knew they were playing the word game, but he had already convinced her. She sipped at her tea, looking him over.

"Well, interesting you mention that. I was planning on making some runs for some little sweets. I have my own shop, though I can't keep up with the demand. I think I'm going to sell everything online, and then ship it. That's why I was glad to hear from you. I need someone who can make just about anything I come up with look like a million bucks."

"Then I'm what you want. I specialize in taking mouthwatering shots of the smallest treats. I just finished a spread for really small donut holes. After the ad ran, they sold out in a day. It's amazing how a good photo sells treats. I do specialize in that type of shot..."

Finishing her tea, she said she'd love to see some samples and talk price, so if he had time, she'd like to show him her shop. Leaving his roll untouched, he picked up the camera, nodded, and she got up and led the way.

Once outside, she asked if he was working for anyone else. He told her he had, but the man who ran things met with a pretty bad accident and everything fell apart. She nodded, saying how anything can happen in certain lines of work, but she took safety precautions. Turning to go into a midtown hotel that held small conference rooms, he followed her, not asking more until she offered to get down to business. There was a sign outside a conference room saying there were going to be photo sessions for child models, and she led him in. The room was empty. While turning on lights she pointed to a small table with two stacking chairs.

"I assume you have some sample work to show. All I can tell you right now is that I specialize in recruiting child models and video talent. I need someone who can take, well, more than flattering pictures of the little things. My photographer decided to stay abroad, and I find I'm in need of someone to replace him. So, let's start with some of your work."

He knew she was going to make a decision on if he was going to play games, or just come out and tell her what he really was best at. He wasn't there to play footsie.

"Sure. Well, based on where I saw your posting, I was sure that you'd want to see these…"

Handing her his phone, he had photos of naked girls having sex, none older than ten. She looked, scrolled through them, nodded at each, then handed him back the phone.

"Your portfolio is impressive. Those are the kind of shots I need. So honest, and you really capture the beauty of such models. You

                                        Innocence Taken

said you worked with someone. Did you find your own talent, or was it where models were brought to you?"

"I don't go out and recruit or solicit. I'm a shooter. Pics or vids. That's it. I like studio work, and I don't want company when I work."

"That works for me. I provide the talent, and then find clients who can afford such luxuries. That's what I do, and you'd do what you do. Now, there is a certain… well… finesse to this type of modeling. Do you sometimes find the models difficult to work with?"

Shaking his head, he looked at her without caution and told her how he liked to work.

"Like you said, you recruit and get them lined up. I expect that they'll all be docile. Given some candy or whatever to keep them good while in front of the camera. So, if not, I wouldn't be able to get the types of shots I just showed you."

"I assure you that they'll all be tame kittens. We have a nice place for them to nap after their hard work, and then they're off to see the world and we find them work that pays well, So, speaking of payment, what are you looking for?"

"A bit of the cut. A decent share. I would expect some for me to work with to build my collection, at least some I can have time alone with. I have specific types and I think that's fair. I'll give you some wonderful shots from my personal portfolio, and the model will get top dollar with those."

Sitting back, she thought about it. She was in need of someone who was smart and sensible. He knew what he wanted and was clear about it. She had told him what he needed to know, and he had done the same. She needed to test him before going further on two matters she was now sensitized to.

"Okay, I know when someone bakes away they want more than a taste of what's going to be sold. One thing I can't have is a mess. Where the treats get broken or aren't good for even the bargain bin. If that's part of the day for you, that's what I don't want."

"I'm not like that. I make things look pretty, and I can't stand when they're not. No waste bin for me. I do everything to make them sell and that's why I get top dollar."

She thought he couldn't have understood her better than if he came out and said it. He seemed to get off on looking and watching. His portfolio showed how well he did that. It was never certain, but the way he looked at her she knew if he wanted to get off, it would be with a real woman who knew what she was doing. He wasn't like Jack. Not a pretty boy or playing the role of photographer. He had a rugged quality and the way he dressed matched his manner. He was strong, certain, direct, and he wore clothes meant for work. They were practical yet well tailored. The jacket or pants didn't hide that he was buff, and where she did get off watching Jack have sex, with him she wouldn't want to just watch. Shaking herself out of a sudden fantasy, she didn't want her judgement clouded with the truth he was her type.

The only other thing she needed to be sure of was that he was who he said he was. There were laws about asking a law enforcement officer if they were that, and they had to answer or a case against her would be thrown out.

"This is a tricky business. You never know who you're dealing with, and I'm sure you understand that I have to protect my clients and my enterprise. So, how do I know you're not a food inspector?"

Nodding, he knew it would be asked. He was ready for such a question, and remained mannered.

"You know, it's both ways. It's impossible to know who is who. I only worked for one guy, and he got offed. Made me run far as I could. You can look up the incident. But, that would be my only reference and he's dead. I just showed you confidential pictures. I took that chance. You can turn me in right now, so I took a chance on you. Now, it's up to you to take a chance on me. I tell you this. Put some models in front of me, and you won't have any doubts. Guys like me, we're not looking for attention, so this is a perfect place for me. Also, if you don't trust me, or you make a move that makes me think you're not for real, I have a Glock in my belt and I've never had a problem using it."

He looked at her, moving his eyes up and down, then added that would be a waste so he hoped that would be the last mention of such a worry both ways. She wasn't acting concerned, and she nodded, saying she admired a man who had everything he needed in his pants. Not using a subtle hint or code speak, she asked him if she could have a look.

Reaching behind him, as he pulled out the Glock, she heard the safety click off as he pointed it right at her head.

"That's how to do it. The last guy was a pussy. The fucker got off by choking girls. He's fertilizing beets near Moscow now. No need to show more. I have one in my bag and I'd show it to you the same way. I asked to be sure, so now we're both sure. So, a 20% cut off of my take, and one pick from each group. Fuck 'em, have them suck your dick, I don't give a fuck what, if most are sold as virgins, so just ass or mouth, but no marks. No fucking with their heads or telling them about what we are or do. Pictures? I get copies. No distributing them anywhere. Buyers don't what what they own on display. They own them, not you. If you can do things like that, I can start you today."

"I'll lay it out. I have my own do and don'ts. I don't make marks, don't go for that sado shit, and I never show my face in shots. You can have any picture I take; my face won't be in them. I know once sold the pics are not for distribution. I'd be pissed if I was a buyer and saw what's mine online. I have a question. The sign outside says up to ten. Anything older? I shoot the little ones as I think they're pure art, but for fucking? Just late teens. I like the fresh skin and being the first."

"Plenty of those. It's the bread-and-butter, but big money isn't going for them. I guess once they got a taste of single digits… it's like a drug. That's what gets them off so they're fucked and we cash in. Teens? Not as much cash as before, but still worth doing. Sure. The teens? Fuck all of them you want. They're so drugged out they don't know what the fuck is going on. Those I have a system to follow. Have shots of each of them giving you head, so just POV. Same cut to you, but a blowjob from everyone of them. They show up for auditions. Too big to snatch. So, you play the game so they don't run out. Woo them with charm and say they're beautiful. You do that, I give them a laced drink, then they'll be sucking your dick. They sell best starting with a pic of a cock in their mouth. It's a big selling point."

"You know what works, so sure. Girl opens her mouth, I get hard, put it in. What's not to like about that? Okay, it all works for me. I know you'll appreciate that like you, I'm a pro, and it's all about money for me. If I want ass or head, I just need look at a bitch and I have her. When do we start?"

Jamie looked at him and knew he wasn't bragging. She could see how his confidence would get him all the women he wanted. She had decided to say yes and have him start.

"We shipped out last night. I'm about to change the sign to teen model auditions. Start this evening. I'm sure for the setup I you have what you need. A simple studio is in the next room. Lights and backdrops, MacBook, port and sync box. You have your camera. It's all ready. Are you?"

"Yeah, for that, always ready… I guess talking about it… I'm down for doing some teen ass and to fuckin' cream their faces. I like the way you work. No bullshit. Get them in, I'll fuck them, take the shots, then the fun part. Sit and watch your bids get high as they'll be must-haves the way I shoot."

Looking at his phone, he acted as if thinking about his schedule. He had made it in faster than he expected, but it was a risky business to be in, and not that many shooters took such chances.

"I'll just hang, get it set up. Jamie, I went through some sick shit in the Congo. Not into guys with rifles aiming at a girl who cried. That shit way of doing things. They were too smart to lose money that way, but I know they would have killed them if it came to that. I'm so glad I'm out of there. Some American ass will be sweet."

Going to the large room with the lighting and gear, he put his camera and tripod down, then looked everything over while glancing to see if Jamie was looking. At first, she was, asking if it was all that was needed. He said it looked great, saying she had all the right things, then looked at her, and this time didn't hide his looking her up and down, asking her to lift her dress as he repeated she had all the right things.

She knew what he meant, and showing him she did, looking at his crotch, she said so did he. With that message, she left.

After that he didn't notice her looking in, but he was sure she had a camera hidden somewhere and the last thing he would do is look for it. His biggest problem was that in a short time he was going to be part of taking pictures of teen girls, they'd be drugged, and he said he wanted to have sex with them. He needed to figure out how to be the creep he said he was, but even undercover, what he'd need to do was sick in his mind. It was always a problem with deep undercover work, and the reason he left field work and started working monitoring trafficking activity online. Even doing that, guys doing such work were questionable to him. He would watch the fresh-out-of-college tech-types who he was sure had never been laid, seeing them with mouths open as they went through sick images or getting stuck on a photo. He didn't see than as different than the men paying for access and hiding behind g-mail accounts. They hid behind agency jobs.

Setting up his camera, he realized he was back in the place he had been many times before, doing the same sick things as the groups he infiltrated.

Thinking it through, he needed go along with it, have sex, take the pictures, and the thought sickened him. He could call it in as what he had done in the past to not engage in sex and ask for a raid. Such a raid would save the group coming in and stop Jamie's operation. That was the only way to not rape the young girls. Attaching a sync cord to the power box for the lights, he'd do something he'd done with success once before. Call in a special CIA team saying one of her buyers gave her up. That would allow him to be taken as well, making it where they were both facing charges.

That seemed to be the best. She would think she was in trouble from one of her clients using her as a bargaining chip. It wouldn't be where she was shut down just before girls started arriving, and he would gain her trust by getting them out of the situation. He needed to call in and lay it out before the teen girls started arriving. It had to be done one way or another, and with this they'd find out more about her operation and her network in Russia. He hadn't expected to be taken in by Jamie so fast. He had monitored her activity enough to know one of her clients. It would be fitting as he was one who had been the representative of the man who bought Angie and Cindy. The man showing up would say they weren't mother and daughter, and she was in for it.

He looked at his watch and he wished he had outlined such a protocol before going deep, but it was a regularly used routine. He just needed to get the buyer's name and the reason back to James. One call would do it, and he would be all set. Knowing the equipment well, he knew he could rig the lighting power box to break a circuit without anything looking other than it simply blew. He'd need a new fuse, and just needed to tell Jamie the box blew, and he'd need to run to the photo supplier, asking which one she used. Without the lights, the photo shoot would look phony. He prayed she didn't have a spare. He needed to make it totally convincing. Attaching a cable, he twisted a prong on the connector, knowing it would cause the breaker to go. He wanted Jamie to see it happen.

Going out where Jamie was working on her laptop, he said he needed her help.

"See you're busy, but if you can spare a minute. I'd like to do a test shot with this light kit. A gray card doesn't think it's a teen girl. If you could stand and let me fire off a few, I'll be all set."

Nodding, he could tell Jamie had been around photoshoots enough to know what he wanted. Closing her laptop, she nodded and walked with him into the other room.

"Yeah, right there with the little black X. I may have to do a few if the lights aren't exactly where they need to be."

She stood, calmly waiting. He didn't look at her, only up at the angle of the lights, then went back to his camera. He attached the sync cord, looked in the lens one time to make sure she was in frame, then using a wireless remote, he took one shot. There was a loud pop from the box, a bit of smoke coming from it.

"What the fuck?"

He went to it, using his hand to wave away the smoke, then pulled the electric cord out of the power strip. He bent over, looking at it as Jamie came to join him. She asked what had happened.

"Well, the fuse… the circuit breaker on this model, it's fried. Maybe a short in my cable, I can't be sure so I just replace the cable and the breaker…"

Taking a pair of pliers from a toolkit next to the power box, he used it to pry the smoking breaker out. It was charred, and there was no doubt it was useless. He looked at it, in the lighting kit toolbox, then at Jamie.

"Didn't expect that. Any backup parts around? Most pros keep extras…"

Standing up, she said she had only what was in the toolbox.

"I've had strobe bulbs pop, so a few of those. I thought I had all the things needed. If it's not in there, no. I set this rig up myself. Can you fix it?"

Standing up, looking at the still smoking breaker, he shook his head to indicate no.

"It did what it's intended to do what it did when it got too much juice. That's why it's called a breaker. They break and that's that."

Shrugging, he told her most any photo supplier would have one, and they should get a few.

"Well, you're the pro. One nearby?"

"Bobs Pro Photo… Yeah, not too far. I'll call to be sure they have some in stock."

"Have enough time before the girls arrive?"

"It's not too late. I don't know their hours, but if they're open, yeah, plenty of time. Just put a new one in, and the only thing that could pop it is the sync cable from the camera. I'll get that too."

He pulled his phone out, called the store, glad they answered, then knelt down to read the model number and ask how many they

Innocence Taken

had. Listening, he asked them to please wait for him, he'd be there in about twenty minutes, tops. Putting his phone away, he turned to Jamie with a look of relief.

"Three in stock. Sync cords are universal so any brand will work. Well, that's a relief."

Looking at her, Jamie said she was glad it happened with her in front of the camera, not a line of girls.

Smiling inside, Mike thought to himself how right she was.

"Be back in a flash, to use a pun. New setup. Things happen. Glad you have the bulbs as that's about the only other thing that can throw a shoot. Gotta run…"

Chapter Thirteen
Man on the Run

"James, got to make this go down fast. I don't have time to talk so here's the deal. I need a grab… I have about ten minutes to lay it out. I got in with the trafficker… Yeah, that's the info I left in case of this. She's the scraper here, does a high volume with model casting and has moved to younger takes… Tonight, she has teens coming in, and I'm suppose to do them and take pictures of me having sex with them for her to send to her clients, all in Russia. She drugs them, and in no time on a private jet to outside of Moscow… I'll find all that out… Yeah, well, the two in the newspaper, for their largest buyer. This is our chance. Have Arnie to play the buyer's guy here, saying the two from the paper were damaged goods and he's out for her to make things right. Have him grab her, and me, and hold us in some warehouse… yeah, that's good. Just him. Tell him to use force and whatever it takes to get the list from her. Yeah, that's it. After about a day, bust us, put her in holding and we scour her PC… The kids tonight will see it's not happening, so they go home. It's gotta go down in under three hours from right now… Is he open… good, if he wants, a second is good, so all he needs is that her partner in Russia is Brian. I heard her on her satellite phone talking about tonight's run. Then, Angies the girl, Cindy's the mom and client tells Brian they aren't related. We're setup at the Allen Midtown, signs are up… She's Jamie, I'm still Mike… Yeah, Arnie provides no info except the buyers wants his money back. Good to get her laptop and when she's wiring, he grabs it. You know the routine… Yeah, we've done more in less time. Once we get the bust, separate us and with all the data I need a jet to Russia, and I'll take it from there… Okay, I'll see you tomorrow. Oh, she has a 45 in her bag and she's good with it, and I'm carrying a Glock in my pants, so I'll come out with it, and he'll know what to do… okay, gotta go."

Shocked he got all of it out as he entered the photo store, he quickly purchased the supplies and made a quick trip back, bag in hand. Jamie was still working on her laptop, looking up to ask him if it was the right stuff.

"Yeah, I'll go check all the wiring first, then see if I can pop the strobes before I call you for the light test. Here's the receipt."

Putting it on the table, she said he'd be reimbursed with pussy.

"Well, I have an LLC, so I'll use it for that, then."

Taking it back, it was just a show that he was business-minded, and flexible. He knew all the cables and connectors were fine, but went through a check as she was most likely watching him. Acting like the sync cable seemed to be the trouble, he threw it in a trash can, then used the new one. Putting the new breaker in, he clicked his camera shutter and the lights popped. Nodding, he threw the extra ones in the toolbox, kept testing the lights, then stopped, satisfied they were working. Going out to Jamie, he said everything was okay, so when she was ready, test shot time.

Watching her get up, he decided to do a full-model shot so the agency would have a current picture of her. He had set the lights up to impress her as well. Standing on the right spot, he said to strike a business-like pose so she could see his style. The way she moved and got into a classic stance he could tell she was once a model. After a few shots, and him suggesting a few moves, they went to the MacBook and looked at the shots. She leaned over, and nodded.

"Those are way better than I expected. Lighting is perfect. Yeah, I'll keep those. Airdrop them to me."

"Jamie, it's easy to see you modeled. Commercial, or porn?"

Laughing, she nodded.

"Oh, never commercial. Too cutthroat and ruthless. Porn when it still had scripts and fashion, now it's just fucking. I still get offers.

Mom parts, you know, all the stepmom and stepdaughter doing dumbass boyfriends. I do some when I need fucked. I get paid, so why not get off and get cash? You do much?"

"Sure. In front and behind the camera. You know, in front, paid with ass fucking. Behind, well, just okay money. I do it for the ass, really. Do that long enough and no matter how sweet the pussy, it's hard to get excited so now, well, this shit does me good. Money's better too."

She raised her dress up, and she wasn't wearing anything under it. She was waxed and she sat on the table, spreading her legs. She didn't say anything, and neither did he. He leaned over and began licking her clit, and she wrapped her legs tight around his head. He knew she was in need as she came quickly, and she stayed open, wanting a second cum. That didn't take much effort either. As she panted from the second cum, she slid down and knelt in front of him and pulled his cock out, and he knew she was a pro. She got him in deep, and worked his balls at the end, licking them as she stroked him, knowing when he was going to cum, putting him in her mouth just in time, sucking it all down.

She got up, smiled, and walked back to the other room as Mike pulled up his pants. His Glock was still there on the ground, and she wasn't using the sex to take it from him. He checked and the clip was still in, his wallet was there as well. It was just sex, and she was good at it. Her body was a surprise as she downplayed her looks and wore clothing that didn't reveal her shape. She seemed satisfied at his skill, and he figured it was somehow her needing to get off, but also to see if he was only aroused by children. He had proven he was good for all types.

Figuring she must have learned the trafficking business while doing porn, he knew most like her had been abused, or often trafficked. He would learn more when they were held captive, but he was already sure she was taking revenge on something she had been through. He decided to put it all to the test and went out to see her.

"Getting sucked off helps me before a shoot. It calms me down a lot. Suck me off again?"

As she nodded, he walked back to the photo room, and took off his pants. She looked at him, and she pulled her dress fully off.

"Fuck me. I need it. I want you to fuck my ass too."

He was amazed at how good her body was. It was all natural, no breast implants, and she looked completely different than when she was playing the hard-assed trafficker. She went to the table, and as he approached, she put him in her mouth to get him hard and had him dripping with slobber. After spitting all she could onto his cock, she got up and leaned over the table so he could do both holes from behind. Rubbing her pussy, he put his fingers in her and she was wet. Putting his cock in, he went full thrust with her calling out to him to fuck her hard as he could. Her whole body rippled with each thrust, and with each she panted, her head sideways on the table, one hand by her mouth as she sucked on her fingers. She started cumming and her eyes rolled up as she put her whole hand in her mouth as she clearly wanted to scream out. After she came, she took her hand out and told him to do her ass.

Putting the head of his cock right under her asshole, he spit on it several times, worked the spit in with the tip of his cock, went right in, and her whole body shook as he went balls deep. She grabbed the other side of the table edge with both hands, moaning and panting, telling him to go harder, harder.

Pulling her ass apart, he spit on his cock as it pulled out a ways, then he slammed it into her. Just as she shouted for him to bang harder, the door burst open and there stood his requested agent, Arnie, large Russian automatic with silencer pointed at the both of them.

Seeing him, Jamie shouted out to him.

"Wait until he cums you motherfucker!"

Chapter Fourteen
Close Quarters

"Finish bitch. I watch. I tape."

Arnie was cold as ice. Holding his gun at them both, he took his phone out of his pocket and held it up to them, a light coming on to show it was recording."

"Fuck bitch, I show Brian you hurt goods."

Mike had already started to cum as Arnie walked in, so pulled out and came on her lower back. He backed up, hands up, and Jamie pulled up from leaning on the table, cum dripping down her ass and legs, looking at Arnie. She didn't seem frightened. She was calm.

"Okay, well, I'm not the goods, so why are you here?"

"Questions? Me to ask, not American bitch slut. Get clothes, I check."

Putting the phone back in his suit coat pocket, Arnie's accent was perfect, and Mike knew his Russian was flawless as he had been a field agent there for 5 years before coming in.

"Back. Move away, be naked. Go against wall."

Hands up, they each slowly backed until they reached the wall. Arnie kicked at Jamie's dress, sending it flying, and it was only the dress, nothing else. Then, kicking at Mike's clothes, the Glock flew out of them and slid on the floor. Arnie kept looking at them as he picked up the Glock and put it in his pocket. He stepped on the clothes looking for anything more. There was an extra clip, and he took that as well. After the search, he kicked all the clothes to them, not saying a word.

As they dressed, Jamie rubbed his cum on her ass and back and let it absorb into her skin. Mike looked at Jamie with a questioning look, as if asking what to do. She shook her head slightly, letting him know now wasn't the time. After they were dressed, Arnie kept his gun aimed on them as he pulled at the studio MacBook and once free of its cables, put it under one arm, then pointed for them to go out to the other room as he moved back far enough to get a shot off if they made any moves.

Moving behind the table, his eyes never left them, nor did the barrel of the gun as he reached down for Jamie's canvas briefcase. He put it on the chair, pulled her MacBook from its cables after closing it, then put both of them in her bag. Reaching in, he pulled out her 45, then put it in his other suit pocket.

"Now, we see how smart American slut and dumbfuck assistant are. If smart, you walk all slow… nice, go out to front side door, no the revolving one, simple one on side, get in back of black car out past door. Close door behind you, that's all you do. Make sound. Make dumb move, I drop both you, get in car and go. Bye bye you, drive away me. We go now. Be smart, I be nice."

Jamie calmly said they would be smart, and she understood what he asked. She turned, nodding to Mike, and as they exited the room, Arnie moved his gun under his suit coat, but ready to pull it out in an instant.

Doing exactly what they were told, they got into the black Tahoe outside, and in the third row was a second man with a semi-automatic pointed to their seats. With a gun behind them, there was little chance of doing more than sit there. Mike knew the man in the third row, and he was also a former agent in Russia, and he was glad to have a second on the mission. Arnie went to drive, saying, "Enjoy ride, you tow, be smart more, keep mouth shut."

The man from behind put a black bag on top of each of their heads, and they understood what was wanted, putting the bags over their heads.

Driving for close to a half hour, after the Tahoe stopped they heard an overhead garage closing, then the sound of Arnie getting out of the front seat and closing his door. Next, he opened the door on Mike's side, and said, "Bags off, get out car."

Once out, Arnie was standing with a large semiautomatic rifle, guarding them until the second man got out of the car. There were two folding chairs in the middle of the open space in what seemed to be an empty warehouse, and there was a small square table between the chairs. Pointing to the chairs with his gun barrel, they each walked slowly to them, then sat down. The second man used a nylon strap to secure their hands, and there was only one light on in the large space, and it was directly over them.

As the second man stood with his gun pointed at them, Arnie pulled a third folding chair out of the darkness and opened it across from them, then went to get Jamie's bag and set it by his side. He looked at them both, shaking his head before he started talking to them.

"Slut bitch, Brian, no happy with you. Brought him shit. Made fool of him."

Jamie looked puzzled, and clearly had no idea what he was talking about. She explained matters to him.

"He inspected everything. All sales final. I have no idea what he could be mad about."

Arnie sat without changing expression.

"Merchandise not from thrift store. Top dollar paid by buyer. You lie, you payback buyer with interest."

Looking at Mike, he could tell she didn't have a clue what he was talking about. She looked to him, changing her attitude.

"Brian knows I stand by my goods. I don't know why the buyer is saying they are not as promised. Can you explain what he says it the problem?"

Arnie was without sympathy, looking disgusted.

"Slut bitch wants me to answer. Want me to suck that man's dick after it leaves ass to? I know just to take you, wait for him say what to do. Buyer say mother is not mother to young bitch. DNA test done. No relation. Said you should test before being cocksucking thief. That's all he say."

Sitting with her eyes wide, she looked shocked. That had her in a bind. A bad one. She asked if she could use her laptop to lookup records, send him what was needed. Mike was glad she asked. Once she logged in, she'd be opening up her contact list, and that's what he needed most. It would take time to work the encrypted file, and all she needed to do was open it. He gently moved his head to Arnie, who knew he was expected to scare her enough to open the file in front of him.

Walking away while the other man guarded them, they could hear him talking in Russian, and just enough to sound like he was asking about it, but not loud enough to hear the words spoken. Walking back, looking more upset, he reached in the bag for her large MacBook. He held it.

"I talk with. He say if proof, send. He say if bullshit, it no be good for you."

Mike knew the call was really to a team ready to burst in and take all of them into federal custody, so as soon as she opened her file, Arnie would hit a button on his phone, and they would break in. The other man went behind her and cut the nylon ties binding her hands. Looking worried and fumbling a bit, Jamie opened her laptop, entered a password, then went to a file and entered several passcodes and the file opened. Mike nodded, and in under a minute the door was busted open and a team with assault rifles flooded in, shouting all hands up, all hands up. They had serious automatic weapons with laser targets on each of their heads.

Rushing at them, the agents went right to them, and the one rushing Jamie pulled the laptop off her lap, leaving it open, and an agent behind her pulled her hands behind her and cuffed her, one did the same to Mike, and agents for Arnie and the other man. The laptop, left on the floor, stayed there as Jamie and the rest were shouted out and pushed towards the door and into a large truck for prisoners. As they were driven away, James, who had on tactical gear and a helmet, reached down and was sure not to close the lid of the laptop, using his camera to take pictures of the screen, scrolling down, taking pictures as all the records were captured just in case the file was timed to close and needing a passcode reentered. He stood, thinking of how well Mike had pulled things together. There were over two hundred names in the contact list. Most were Russian, but there were also many prominent US government and business leaders there. It was a jackpot, and the laptop would have more to examine.

The ruse with Jamie and Mike continued as they were brought to a federal building with high security. They watched each other being processed, printed, scanned, and stripped then given orange overalls. Jamie kept looking at Mike, shaking her head to indicate say nothing, and he nodded back. She watched as he was taken away, and then she was taken in the other direction and put in an interrogation room. From that point on, she wouldn't see him again. Mike was being taken to a changing area where he put his clothes back on after a shower, and then went to James' office where Mike sat as they smiled at each other.

"There it is. All open and ready for the nerds to go at. Good job, Mike. And it happened so fast. I took shots of the contacts. I'm sure this is what you wanted. The whole list will be on the portal for you, but she brings girls to Brain, he sells them. The two you want, sold to a prince in the Middle East. A sheik. They're still at

Brian's according to the record, for another week. So, this is where you'll find the two you want first. The jet's ready for you. I don't even want to ask what you'll do once there. Need anything?"

"I've been thinking it through. I think an account number that will wire as much as I punch in. If they are at risk, I'll buy them. Anything more, too risky. It also establishes a transaction, a trail. It will get me to the final buyer. What we need is the name of the Arabian buyer. Hard to do without it, but if I need to, I can dance around it. Once down, a large limo and our top asset as my guard. Think you can do that?"

Writing it all down, he said it was no problem, but the name of the final buyer from Jamie may not be easy. She may not even know it.

"James, if she doesn't, she'll know who does. She'll give you the name to save her own ass."

Laughing, James was shaking his head, Mike asking him what could possibly be funny.

"Oh, sorry, Mike. Really. Just that Arnie had those pictures for evidence, and as I looked at them he said you sure liked doing her ass, so…"

"Jeez! You know how it goes. Deep cover."

"Mike, he said that too. You were deep as you could get!"

"Where's he at? I want him to know I'm going to say he was perving on it before interrupting us in my report!"

"Mike, Mike. After all that, it's good to laugh a little. And hey, I saw the strip search, it was a really nice…"

Turning, leaving with the door slamming, James had enjoyed

teasing him. It would give him something to think about on the flight and admit to himself that he enjoyed it. She was an attractive woman, and that's why he reacted so strongly.

Not really as upset at James as he acted, he knew it was to distract him. He was facing a tough situation, and as he thought about it, he knew they were right. He had enjoyed sex with her. He could still hear her screaming out to fuck her harder, and he hadn't held back as it was immensely exciting. Watching her eyes look up at him as she gave him head was still in his mind, and he shook his head, knowing that was the wrong thing to be liking. She was a woman, but one who sold children and teens. It worried him that she aroused him. He shouldn't have been able to even get hard with such a sick woman.

But, he had.

Chapter Fifteen
Just Desserts

"Mom… Oh, my God. Oh, I'm so sorry!"

Shivering in terror, inconsolable, eyes burning from crying, Angie was coming fully out of her drugged state. The reality of what had happened to them was hitting her full force. Life at the trailer park had been horrible, but being trafficked was beyond a nightmare and she couldn't comprehend how it all happened. It was all a blur, and she was gasping for air as Cindy hugged her, telling her to slow down, breathe slow.

"Angie… Right now, we need to get okay. We were drugged and it's still in us. I don't know where we are, but we need to calm down and figure it all out…"

Looking around, they were in a dark room, and they seemed to be sitting on carpeting, leaning against what felt like a bed. Cindy wondered who else was there with them. She patted Angie on her back as she hugged her, then told her she wanted to see if she could find a light, so stay put. Angie whimpered she wouldn't move, and she was so afraid.

"It'll be better if I can turn on a light… See where we are."

Letting go of Angie, she felt the bed against her back, and thought how most beds had a bedside table at the head, and most had a lamp on them. Using her hand to follow the bed, she only crawled a few feet, and as she thought, there was a cabinet — the type next to most beds. Using her hand, she rubbed it up the cabinet, then she knelt up. There was a lamp on it. Riding her hand up its curved shaped, she felt the familiar chain pull for the bulb, and pulled it.

Filling the dark with light, the lamp worked. She saw Angie on the floor, looking up with surprise at her. Turning, Cindy saw they were in a nice room with a large bed in the middle, having cabinets with lamps on each side. The bed had pillows and an embroidered duvet covering a comforter. There was a dresser across from the bed, and there was an open door to a bathroom. Looking around, she saw a door she assumed must be to the hall, but there were no windows. There was a large flat-panel TV and paintings on the wall of landscapes. In the far corner were two stuffed easy chairs, a table between them, and another lamp. On the table was bottled water and a tray with domed plates, meaning food under them.

"Angie, get up. Take a look. It's a regular room. A nice room."

Having trouble getting up, Cindy went to her to help, and she was still sobbing. Slowly leading her to the bathroom, she took her to the sink, adjusted two handles to get the water tepid, leaned her over while telling her to splash water on her face. Shaking, Angie started splashing it on herself, and as she was bent over, Cindy looked in the mirror above the sink, seeing herself naked, as was Angie. She looked around the bathroom. There were towels, and she was glad to see there were two terrycloth robes with belts. She felt relief as wherever they were, they were being treated with basics needed to get better.

Going to a walk-in shower, it was tiled and had shower heads on three sides and from above. The knob to run the water was just as she stepped in. Turned it on, soon it was nicely warm. There was a ledge inside that had soap and shampoo, and she thought what they needed most was to get clean, washing the filth of what had happened to them away. She kept turning the faucet and kept feeling the water until it was nicely hot, then stepped out to get Angie.

They both were still in the horrible black nylons. She pulled hers off, throwing them in a wastebasket, and Angie had stopped splashing her face and was watching. Cindy knelt down in front of her and pulled each nylon off as Angie shook while stepping out of them. Putting her arm around her, she led Angie to the

                                    Innocence Taken

running shower and went in with her, started washing her, then shampooing her hair. She went slowly and could see that she didn't have any bruises and the shower was helping. As she went to rinse her hair, Angie looked at her.

"I think I can do that. I'll shampoo it again, then let me do your hair."

That was wonderful for Cindy to hear. They both were full of lather and soap, and they washed each other and soon felt clean and fully awake. The hot water seemed to be washing away the effects of the drug they were given. After each rinsed off, they hugged each other and Cindy told Angie they were okay, and to keep a positive mind. It was important to not be afraid.

Cindy, reaching for towels, felt they were large and fluffy enough to get their bodies and hair dry. Stepping out of the shower, Angie pointed to a shelf above the sink having a comb and a brush. Cindy took one of the robes and held it for Angie to put on, then did the same for herself. Taking the comb, she ran it through Angie's hair, and once free from tangles and looking good, she did her own hair. She saw she looked run down, but she felt clean and fresh. There wasn't a hair dryer they could find, so Cindy said it was air dry time. There was a medicine cabinet, and they both were surprised as it had toothpaste, toothbrushes, deodorant, and some aspirin. On the top shelf were tampons. Thinking all that was good, it also made Cindy realize that the room was used for women being held as it had all the basics women needed. That thought upset her, though she didn't let on to Angie. All the products had names and directions in Russian, and that let her understand where they were.

"Well, that sure helped. And guess what? I think there's food. Let's take a look."

Taking Angie by the hand, they each sat on a stuffed chair, then looked at what was under the silver domes on the tray. Each plate had sliced ham, cheese, and baby carrots. It was a cold plate, but there was plenty on each. Also on the tray was bread, along with plastic forks and knives. There were two clear plastic cups next to the bottled water, so being hungry, they both started to eat.

"This will help with that drugged feeling. Do you still feel woozy?"

Angie shook her head, saying not so much. She looking about to cry, Cindy decided to see if she could help her feel a bit hopeful.

"Well, let's take our time eating. If we eat too fast, we could get sick. I don't know how long we were out, but I sure am starving. Okay, yes, just nibble, like me. So, when we first woke up, I thought we were in some prison or dungeon, so this was a surprise. I think it means whoever took us doesn't want to hurt us now, so that's good. They have stuff for us to get cleaned up and the bed to sleep in is nice. I didn't look in the closet…"

Looking, Angie saw two doors that slid to open and got up to see if anything was inside. It was a closet, and inside were simple nightgowns, dresses that looked close to their size, underwear and socks, even shoes. The dresses were long and had long sleeves and buttons up to the neck in front. The shoes were simple flats, and the socks were black knee-highs made of cotton. She pulled each one out and showed them to Cindy, who nodded, understanding they were for modest dressing, not to be sexy. She told her that was good but come back and eat. Angie looked around as she came back, then sat.

"No window, and I would guess that door is locked. We're prisoners, mom!"

"Sweetie, we are. I know that. But, right now, we need to get some food in us and stay smart. Calm. I want to know what you remember. I mean, from the time you blacked out…"

Eating a carrot, Angie closed her eyes and tried to put her

memories together. Opening them, she was starting to recall things.

"Well, we went to get the pictures of me done. That Vlad guy, he said you were pretty like me, and took pictures of us together… Mom, I was so excited when we were getting our pictures taken… then, we sat down with him… and that Jamie woman. We drank some really sweet iced tea. Then, not much more. I just was happy as can be, then felt all kinds of bumps and heard noises but I was asleep but kind of awake. Do you remember all that?"

Nodding, she was sipping the water, and a fear shot through her that the water may be drugged, but she stopped worrying. It was just water. No funny taste and no reason to have food and water if whoever was holding them wanted them asleep in a drugged state again.

"Pretty much the same things. That, and hearing some talking, but I couldn't understand it all. And it was Russian. Then next, I remember seeing that Jamie by my feet, and I felt a rush go through me. I think she injected something… in my foot…"

Pulling her foot up to examine, she looked it over, then looked between her toes. She told Angie to take a look. There was a bruised area from where she had been injected. She asked Angie to see if she had it too. Looking, Angie showed her she had the same thing. Cindy nodded.

"Yeah… It's getting clearer. I guess the tea had drugs to really knock us out. Then, she injected something to make us wake up, but not all the way. Just enough to stand. I remember wondering who I was… it was really frightening. And then, once I could stand… and you could stand, some men took us to a stage thing. Just one light, above us. And all we had on were those icky nylons, and we were holding each other. Do you remember any of that?"

Angie, shaking, clutched at herself as if to hide her body like when they were on the stage.

"Mom, now, yeah, I do. Feeling like we were like strippers or something, because there were men cheering and clapping… and then, oh, it was horrible… those men, from out of nowhere… from out of the black, they came up to us and started touching us!"

Breaking out in tears and panic, Cindy took her water cup and held it to her mouth, telling her to keep calm and quiet, to drink some water. Angie looked up at her and Cindy's heart sank seeing the look on her face but knew she had to be strong for her. She helped hold the cup, and the water helped. She decided to not to ask her more. She would tell she recalled.

"Okay, just nibble some more on the food, and I'll tell you what I remember about that. Yeah, it was a lot of short, fat men… all with cigarettes… oh, it was full of cigarette smoke. In Russia, they still smoke like crazy, and it stinks so bad. Yes, they were rubbing us, inspecting us like we were cattle or something. Then, they were gone, just as fast, then… yeah… one man came up to Jamie, and they talked about us, but I didn't hear. After that, someone took us to a big black car and we were in the back seat… Oh, then, you couldn't see. I'm glad you didn't. It was not something to ever see."

Angie looked at her, eyes wide, asking what she saw over and over. Cindy thought about it, and she needed to tell her as it was a warning of who was holding them captive.

"I was still only half awake, but I saw something that was a nightmare. Now, Angie, I'm only going to tell you this because no matter what, we play along. We don't fight or put up a struggle or show we're angry. Okay? We can't trust anyone, no matter how they treat us. These are not okay people. We're in this nice room for a reason, and don't let that make it where we're okay yet. Do you understand?"

Looking as frightened as before, even more so, Angie wanted to know what they faced.

                                         Innocence Taken

'Okay, we need to be smart. You were still really out, and I kept wondering what was going on, where we were, so I was looking out the window. I watched as two men walked Vlad, that photographer, onto the stage we had been on, just like they did us. They were on each side of him, holding his arms so he couldn't get away. And that Jamie, she stood in front of him, giving some kind of talk to the stinky men... a speech or something, and then... this, you just have to deal with, I watched as she took a shiny gun, a big one, out of her bag. Then she turned around and shot him in the head. Just like that. It was horrible, and she was cold as ice. I remember, as horrible as it was to see, even worse, she whipped around and held her arms up, like a winner in a race... I passed out. It was too much to see. Next, I was here, waking up with you. That's why I need to tell you... These people, I mean, Jamie... and those men, they're bad, they kill. So, we don't do things to make them mad at us. You need to understand that."

Crying, shaking her head, Angie let it all sink in. She ate some ham, drank some water, then slowly nodded her head.

"Mom, I understand. They may act nice, but they aren't. That Vlad, he was nice to us. Do you think he was bad? One of them?"

Impressed Angie was asking that, Cindy nodded.

"Yes, I think he was bad. He must have done something even the bad men thought was horrible. Did something that made Jamie kill him like that. He was there when we were drugged. He was part of it all. He spoke Russian, but I don't think he was. I could tell. His accent was not real. Not even like Americans who came to the Ukraine and learned a bit to sound like they're from there. He was American, and all the being so nice... that was phony to get us to trust him."

Eating more, Angie was upset, but Cindy saw she was thinking.

"Mom? What is all this? I mean, the model audition thing, taking pictures and saying they had work for me… oh, remember, in the agreement… It said work overseas! We're overseas. That's what that meant."

Being an escort, and having almost all Russian clients, she had heard stories. Yorgi had warned her that it sounded like a nasty business. She had a good idea of what was going on. She needed to tell Angie, and they needed to prepare for things to come.

"I think I know. Some of my guys, well, they know what people do to make lots of money if they can. It all makes sense now, and I'm so sorry I didn't figure it out before you went to that phony audition. See, men… well… they get really, really messed up. I mean when it comes to sex. Some, and you know about this from the news and all, some men like little girls… little boys too for many of them… and it's not only sick, but also against the law. And no mom is going to let her little girl have sex with anyone, let alone sick men like that. So, those men, pedophiles they're called, they look at pictures of little girls naked, or worse, having sex with grown men. It's really sick sick sick. But that's not enough. Some, they take them off the street or tempt them into their car for some reason, then they keep them to have sex with. They mostly get caught and are put away, but the little girls are either dead, or screwed up bad for life…"

Looking at Angie, she saw the pure horror of what she was saying. She asked her if she had read about that or heard of some of it sometimes on the news. Angie slowly nodded her head, saying she thought that was just a couple of weird guys, but didn't know it was a big thing.

"Well, like I said, those are just sick perverts, and they do terrible things and hopefully most get caught. But it doesn't stop there. You know, all kinds of men get like that. Poor ones like on the news, but rich ones too. And that's the worst. Rich guys with money who are sick too… They get away with everything, especially this stuff. They have lots of money, and they pay for guys to kidnap young girls… little tiny girls too, and they buy them. Buy them like a thing. A sex doll. It's all secret, and they can be famous men, politicians, movie stars, company CEOs, anyone with money. They know the money can get them what they want. So, they buy little kids for sex… and then… well… who knows what happens to the little girls. They aren't heard from again. In things I read, the same seller takes them and sells them again somewhere else, over and over. They're sex slaves. They use drugs on them, all kinds of threats."

Cindy took some water. Angie sat, stunned, shocked, but knew she was hearing the truth as her mom wouldn't make things up. She had just heard her mom tell her how her parents had done all those things in the Ukraine, and why they lived in the trailer park. She didn't want to upset her mom, but she wanted to understand if that's what had happened to them. The same as her parents did when she was growing up. She need to ask, and it was hard to do.

"Mom, you just told me about your parents when you grew up. All the things you just said, isn't that what they did?"

"Angie, yes. That's what is so upsetting to me right now. That what I've been hiding us from. So, yes, that's what my parents did in the Ukraine. It's just so unfair. We're like the ones my dad used to sell. I was eating food and had nice clothes from all that. Oh, my God. I can't get escape all that!"

She was crying, realizing she was back in the world her mother fought to get her free from. She stopped crying and needed to finish telling it all.

"So, I know how it all works. But it's gotten worse. All over the world. Now, all of that? It's called sex trafficking. Buying, selling, abusing, kidnapping, killing. It's a big money business. So, that Jamie? She's a sex trafficker. She gets girls, like you, with the hope of being a model. Then you show up, get drugged, and nobody hears from you again. They love girls your age and from bad places like Aurora as they aren't paid attention to by the police as girls your age often runaway. Oh... oh, my God! The name! Runaway Elite. Perfect. I thought it was a play on being a runway model... runaway success. How could I have missed that? Well, and that Vlad, he took pictures, like of you, and she must have sent them to her clients and got them interested in you. I'm sure she was just planning on trafficking you, then with me there, well, we look so alike... and we're mother and daughter, I'm sure we went for a whole lot of money. And that's what happened, I'm sure. We're being sold to some rich, really sicko man who wants to do a mom and daughter."

As she finished getting it all said to warn Angie, she went to her, hugged her hard and they both broke down crying. Cindy knew it was all true. It was what Yorgi was hinting at, not wanting to scare her. It happened so fast. She understood that getting in and out of town quickly was part of how it worked. She hated telling all of it to Angie, but she needed to know to protect herself. If she tried to run, or tell people, she'd be killed or kept with someone who would keep her drugged.

Sitting in the chair, Angie kneeling and holding her, she felt a hopelessness flood over her. She knew such things went on from her own family history, and she often wondered how it could be where the world knew but did nothing to stop it. The news about a rich man who blackmailed presidents and famous people had been on the news for a long time, but nobody was charged. None of the famous people were ever arrested. Finally, the trafficker was put in prison, but he somehow managed to hang himself. She thought of Vlad being shot. When she heard the news, she was sure he hadn't hung himself. The powerful men wanted to shut him up, and that did it.

Just as she thought about that, the door leading out of the room opened and she jumped. It was a woman wearing an apron. Older, motherly, she quietly came in with a tray and nodded at Cindy. At the door stood a large man, hands folded in front of him, wearing

Innocence Taken

a dark suit, not smiling. He was making sure nothing happened and that they wouldn't get out of the room. The woman set the tray on the dresser, then took all the things from the food they had eaten, put it on the dresser, then put the new tray down on the table along with another large bottle of water. She had a pad of paper in her apron, and she put the pad on the dresser along with a crayon, turned to Angie, then speaking in Russian said to write down anything else they may need, and slip the paper under the door if so. She took the first tray, went out the door, the man closed it, then she heard a lock being turned.

Cindy went and sat in her chair. Lifting the dome on the tray, it had a variety of cakes, cookies, and some candy. Angie looked at it, then at Cindy.

"Dessert. Like us."

Cindy understood her comment. That's all they were. Some dessert for some rich man above the law and devoid of any morals. She thought of how sad the world was. It was the men in charge, the ones who could do something to help stop such sick acts who were hiding it and taking advantage of it. She grew angry. She looked over at Angie who was holding her stomach, saying she needed to use the bathroom. She nodded, saying take her time.

Closing the door behind her, Cindy thought about each thing that had happened and was remembering little snippets that seemed to have happened, but she couldn't really put them together. That changed as she heard a yell, then wailing, from Angie in the bathroom. She rushed to the door and went in, seeing Angie with toilet paper red with blood. She about fainted, but then the little memories became all too real. Asking Angie which hole, she heard a wail, Angie crying out it was from behind.

She had Angie stand up, and she was in a total panic. She examined her and saw what had actually happened. She had been penetrated anally, and when trying to go it stretched her in a way where forced entry had torn her in places, and they rips began bleeding. She was kneeling, feeling faint. It was no time to do that, and she needed to help Angie. Getting up, she went into the medicine cabinet and got a tampon, and told her to put it in, which she did with hands trembling.

"Mom! It's not my time yet and it's coming out my butt!"

Wadding some toilet paper, she said if she had to go, go, even if there was blood, just let it out, then put the paper there, then panties to help hold it in place. Angie was looking at her, shaking. Keeping calm, Cindy helped her through it. She said she'd give her some privacy and get the panties for her. She closed the door, went to the closet, got them, then knocked on the door and just put her hand through to hand them to her.

Giving her time and privacy, Cindy was flooded with a memory of both her and Angie laying on their sides, on the floor, and being raped by Vlad. He hadn't cum in them, and she was plenty used to such penetration so didn't even feel anything, but it was a first for Angie, and anal sex done roughly made her glad Angie had been knocked out. It didn't seem he had vaginal sex. Then, she shook, realizing her daughter had been raped no matter where, they wanted her to be sold as a virgin, and it was all horrific. She decided not to tell her, just saying it must have been from when they were being inspected. She saw no point in adding to her trauma.

It was then that seeing Vlad made sense to her. They were a top-dollar item, and Vlad had sex with them. That could have blown the price, or the sale. Angie was offered as a virgin. Jamie couldn't allow him to have vaginal sex, so he had anal sex, and that's why she shot him. He had messed with a rich man's property.

Property. That's what they were now. Someone's property. Bought, bill of sale, someone's to own. Nothing more than something to gloat over, and brag to rich friends about. Maybe pass around as an award or a prize. She didn't know how sick such men were, but she was sure of only one thing.

They would soon find out.

Chapter Sixteen
Rushin'

"Hello, Yorgi? I'm a federal agent working on finding the two women you reported to the *Aurora Light*. If you have some time this morning, I would appreciate speaking with you about them. It would help my efforts in tracking them."

Leaning forward over his desk, Yorgi had a copy of the newspaper article in front of him, and it hurt him to look at. He secretly loved Cindy, but knew he was too old for her and giving the pictures to the local paper was his way of showing he cared when the world around him didn't. The police had not called or visited him for any information, and he was surprised to hear anyone had interest in two unimportant ones living in a trailer park.

"Yes, time I have for this. I put all else aside. But, I must ask you provide proof you are federal agent. Not to be rude, just afraid ones who took may be out to stop me. That, can you do?"

"Certainly. I'll give you my real name and badge number, then you can call to verify if you wish. I understand. I am hoping to act fast, so if I stopped by now, would that be alright?"

"As I say, yes, this important to me. But please, your name? And what is number of your agency?"

After providing what was asked, Mike told James he was going to meet with the lawyer who reported them missing. James shrugged.

"Ah, hell, Mike. I was about to ask you how deeply you got involved…"

Not resisting chuckling due to the sincere look on James' face, he said it was true, he was in deep with Jamie, but that wasn't it.

"No. The issue is this. The girl and mom? They don't exist. At least not with social security, IRS, immigration… nothing on the girl being in school. I looked, had Janis run it every way possible. If I pull them out of Russia, the thing is how to get them back in the US. My guess is they're illegals, and they've hid since getting here. The lawyer is my best hope to find out the whole story if he knows it. I get the feeling he does. I go by the book. Doing a raid on foreign soil for a non-citizen? I don't think you can sign off on that one."

"Mike, yeah, good thinking, and I understand now. Yeah, see what he knows. I don't care either way. We have the woman, and we'll work it where she identifies them from pictures. Maybe. If they aren't legal, we get them legal or say we thought they were, and the records were screwed up. Leave that to me but get on it and get on the jet. Time's the real enemy right now. Let me know how it goes."

Figuring that it was more than a question of if they were legal, the lawyer may know something more than they were missing. He sensed it when talking to him. By now, he figured Yorgi had called headquarters and had gotten a description of him, or at least confirmation.

Aurora was a hellhole, and he hated any time spent there. Yorgi was in an old downtown that still had a few stores and offices open only as there was a riverboat casino there. The stores were mostly gone, but it had eateries, bars, and some shady motels, the emphasis on the shady. The buildings were classics and still looked in good condition. Yorgi's office was in a two-story red brick professional building with a real estate agent on the ground floor. Walking up the stairs, it was one of the rare times he felt any warmth in the decaying town. Everything was in perfect repair, and there was a warmth he admired. Knocking first on the glass door panel, he entered. It was a large room full of file cabinets, and Yorgi getting up from behind a huge old desk. With wood paneled walls and frames with diplomas, he wished all lawyers had such surroundings.

Yorgi held out his hand, greeting him with warmth.

"Mike, you are he? Please, to show me ID, that is all I need."

"Here you are. It's good to check, and I appreciate your taking time to see me. Mind if I sit down?

Putting his hand out to the two chairs in front of his desk, as Mike sat, he took the other chair to face him on the same side.

"Yorgi, as mentioned, I have some questions regarding the disappearance of the two in the paper. It said one was the mother, the other her daughter. Were they clients of yours?"

Staring at him, his face looking sad, Yorgi had decided that Cindy's occupation may be a factor in her going missing, among other possibilities, so spoke candidly.

"Mike, I want only you should find them, and I will tell you confidences. No, she no client. I am client of hers."

Surprised at his honesty, Mike was grateful for it. He had no wish to judge him or the missing woman.

"I understand. She was someone you had company with, but personally, not legally."

"Mike, that is kind way to put it. Yes. I think most loving of her. She had hard start in life. Her father… he bad man, raped her when very young girl. She fled to America, with mother, brother. Brother threatened mother, she returned to Ukraine. Brother, ruined in head, killed himself. She, you know, hid. Stayed quiet, never became citizen. It happen for reasons, her, to protect her little girl. No citizen, no job to have. So, she become, as they say here, escort. But no pimp, just her, and she is good woman."

Thinking how that explained no records, he also knew that with

     Innocence Taken

the right help, she could explain the circumstances and both she and her daughter could be naturalized citizens.

"Did you offer to help her with becoming a citizen? I see on your lobby card you do immigration work."

"Yes, many times, I say it was fear, not wish to do wrong. But, she still afraid. She had customers, like me, but her girl, I told her if she no go school, it would be hard life here, did she wish her be escort too? I think she was getting ready to tell story. Wanted daughter to work, test it out. She told me Angie, daughter, had audition to become model. Big photo thing. Then, she no show. I worry. Call. No answer. Not in trailer where she live. Nothing. So, I had photo of girl from audition, one of her she used as escort, and called paper. Now, I have told you all. The police, not safe to report someone with no history, you understand."

"Yes, and it was me calling you, and I don't care if she's illegal. I care about where she was taken. I've shut the photo audition business down, and the woman who ran it is in custody, but it will take time to get her to tell us much. I have a list she made of her clients in Russia. That's why I'm here. I'm not asking you to tell me who, but I assume you work with people from Russia… ones coming here to escape. Prostitutes, drug dealers… traffickers. I am saying you help people there, and I know you do help them. But I assume when they come to you, they tell you who they are running from. Would that be correct?"

Mike watched Yorgi carefully, and he didn't flinch. He showed a subtle anger at hearing it all. He dealt with people who somehow were cast out, or escaped from all of those horrors, and he may know of the traffickers.

"That is what I do, and people, yes, tell me terrible men who do terrible things. That is my worry. Russian women, very beautiful, most beautiful in world many are. But rich men there, they like ones from here. Young ones. Little malenka baby ones. They send girls here, traffickers here send girls there. They want younger and younger. Big money. Russian and Ukrainian ones sent here? You heard of types, yes? Mail order brides? Get married, take money, divorce, now citizens. Big business here. The other way? Not bride. Slave, for sex. Worse than hookers. Property. I worry that that is for Cindy, her daughter too. So, you have list? I have heard of worst ones. Maybe I see names on list."

Taking out a sheet with a list of names from Jamie's contacts, he handed it to Yorgi, with a slight worry. Yorgi may be connected, but watching him, he was seeing his reaction, and he was showing his hatred. He laid the paper down on his desk and pointed to three names.

"This man, he worst of them. Most money, he buy girls, not for him, he sell them all over world. He is broker, if you think it that way. With ones such as Cindy and her girl, he would be one who could pay most. These too, they are rich. Oligarchs. They would buy for self. Keep. But, high price, they may, may not. If top man I point to, there, they could no outbid him."

Mike would call it in and get deep background on the top pick. He got up, said he was most grateful for the help, and if he had news, he would let him know. Yorgi held up his finger, then handed him a business card and a holy card of the Virgin Mary holding the Christ child, ornate with gold leaf.

He thought about it as he drove. Getting the women would mean getting the largest trafficker. If he did it right, the man could turn on his clients all over the world and expose a large trafficking network and who was behind it. At first it was some need to save the poor women, but now it was saving as many victims of trafficking as possible, and this would be a huge win. He was first going to go alone and do what he did best — break in and steal the victims away. To get the man, he would need help. He would need to do more than shoot him or threaten him. He had to go all out and force him to surrender his clients' information and verify

Innocence Taken

it. It was possible to do with the right intel on the man, so he called James and laid it all out.

"James, hold on as this is going to be intense, but I think we have a good shot here at more than getting the mother and daughter out. The lawyer, he looked at the list from Jamie's computer. He works with people who were trafficked in Russia and escaped to here. He pointed out the largest of them, and I'm sure that's who has them. We need to move fast, and I'm going to do what I do best. Persuade the bastard to hand me his list of buyers. You can take odds and win big saying they're all over, presidents, and the rich. That's worth doing it this way. Now, I have my reasons, but I want you to tell Jamie who I am. Yeah, I was once a photographer, but I'm a field agent and I'm going to get the women — and she's coming with."

"Mike! Are you serious? Reveal yourself? And going in with just her? Wait a minute, is she going to be on your side, or his? A trade? What?"

"You'll understand. I have my intuition, and she will want to take the man down. She'll be with us on this. Go in, talk to her, tell her the basics, and work it where she knows it's that or life outside where she's not going to last a day."

"Mike, it's short notice for a risky run. I've already put in the deep background request, and it'll be in your cloud folder. Are you sure you want to move this fast? You can grab the women, then go back another time."

"James, with Jamie out of touch, he'll learn soon enough we have her and will be alerted. She knows too much, and who knows who he has here watching her. The Russian gangs will do that for free or some exchange. I think it's now. We know it's him, and you can tell Jamie we are going to pay him a visit, maybe say we we're thinking of taking her with as bait. See what she does. And no, no jokes about what kind of bait I use. This is not the time for that."

"Wasn't going there. So, I talk with her. Lay it all out. Let her know she's… almost said it… ah, hell, I will… she's fucked. That you're on the way there with her as a way in the door. She'll know her days are few as the gangs here will get a contract for her even if we take him. Word spreads. So, a team. They have a lot of muscle. We can't send an army. He has his kinks, I'm sure. Listen, let me talk to your favorite gal… now come on… that was fair as she's your way in right now… I'll talk to her and explain she has a choice. Be part of the take, or we let her loose after you're done and she's not going to last long. And if she says she'd turn on him…. Wanted to come with but is still on his side? You could take her out… there I go again; you can take her down if she does anything to spoil it. I think she's smart, and I think she has no allegiance. If she turns, would you go for that? It's a good way in."

Mike kept thinking of how his impression of her when doing her was she had been a victim, most likely of trafficking. He decided to tell James what he thought was best.

"James, do it this way. Go in, tell her I know the bastard had trafficked her, and this is her one chance to take him down for doing it. See what she does. How she looks… acts. If I'm right, you'll see her turn. If not, she'll keep up the tough bitch act. Call me soon, okay?"

Thinking it through, he was too experienced with hurt people to not pick up the signs. Her business in the US was not an inspired idea one day. She had a large client list, a strategy that worked, had run under the radar, and she made a ton of money but didn't act or look like it. She worked the trafficking herself. She was on the ground, not in some mansion. His guess was she was still under the control of the trafficker he identified with Yorgi's help. If so, this was her one chance to pay him back and get free from him. Now, it was a matter of how groomed and brainwashed she was. When he had sex with her, she was looking for more than a climax. She needed someone who didn't pay to do her. She wanted to be valued. Vlad had cheated on her, and he thought that was the real reason she took him down.

Going into a coffee shop, he decided to get a danish and some coffee. He realized that was what he ordered when he first met her. This time he ate it as he waited for a call from James. After a refill, his secure phone rang, and it was James.

"You are way too fucking smart. I told her flat out you knew she had been turned out by him, and that she was still his to control. She sat there, and you should have seen her. She started shaking and she started screaming his name and thrashing about. I told her you were headed to take him down, and she'd either be there to do it with you, or she'd be on the streets for his goons to get. That stopped her cold. She asked a few questions, and I was straight about your plan, and that you knew she was still doing what he said. I told her the truth. I told her you saw through her when you had sex, and this was her only chance to get free. She sat, tears rolling down, but with a look I could bank on, said yes. I tell you, Mike, it's still a risk. With that shit done to her? She could turn on you. That head fuck stuff goes way deep. It's your call. Jet's ready, papers for her by the time she gets fixed up. Need to call back?"

"James, good job. You did it the same as I would have. You know, I can see that in people. I'm back in the field, and if she sides with him, then she's on his side. Have our guy there set up a meeting with him. I'm looking for a steady flow of under tens, price no object. He'll come. Confirm it with me. I'll be there soon to pick her up. Give her everything but a gun. Make sure she looks good. Business suit. Have Janis fix her up if needed. So, a half hour. I'll be in the garage, walk her down with Brooks just in case… okay. Man, you are the only one who would do all this. Thanks."

Shaking his head, he couldn't believe he'd be with Jamie on a jet to Moscow or that she was what he intuitively thought she was. There'd be time to talk on the flight. He just hoped she didn't want to go to the bed in back and fuck him again. Then, he thought again, and hoped she would.

Chapter Seventeen
When Worlds Collide

Riding to headquarters Mike was lost in memories. Thinking about why he had any sympathy for Jamie, and why he was driven to rescue two women out of the thousands who go missing each month was sending him back to the reasons why. He had been in therapy when he asked for a transfer out of field work four years ago. He had sessions with a psychologist who hated therapy. He didn't think sitting and asking questions about feelings did anything except get the therapist session money. His approach was head-on, asking what the problem was and what the fuck you going to do about it.

He knew what he was doing was exactly that. Approaching a problem and doing something about it. He could have watched events unfold, contribute as part of a team, felt bad for victims, and been a typical agent. Let the wrongs of the world take place and cherry pick who to go after. Never get in where the victims were or know what they went through. He thought of his first session with Charles, his therapist.

"Okay Mike, I read you history, and I don't care much about the past as much as about right now. But, it's a place to start. So, you grew up pretty nice. Small town in Michigan on the lake. Parents understanding, had a sister, two years apart. You went to Chicago, degree from the Art Institute in photography, then were a "glamour" photographer. What exactly the fuck is a glamour photographer?"

"It's almost all studio work. Fashion models, cosmetic models. I'd work for magazines or ad agencies and take pictures of tall skinny girls. What the world thinks of as glamorous, not me."

"Good at it?"

"Oh yeah. I guarantee you've seen my work at some point. On a

                                    Innocence Taken

magazine cover at a grocery store checkout. On a billboard. I was in demand and making a lot of money."

"Like it?"

"Yes, loved it. I liked being really good at it. The best at it."

"So, what was better? Doing the work, or being best at it?"

"Being the best."

"Okay, you were the best, had work, liked the work, then you leave and join the agency to start as a field agent. Are you the best field agent?"

"That's what they tell me."

"What if you weren't the best?"

"I keep doing what it takes to be that."

"Mike, I think right now you can face up about being the best at something is what is important to you. So, I hear that, and I am supposed to ask you why. I don't fucking care why. It's just how you are. We can spend years on that shit. Nothing wrong with wanting to be really good at what you do. The jump from taking pictures of beautiful women to being an agent, and now wanting to stop doing field work and sit in the office is why you're here, right?"

"I guess so."

"Mike, I don't want to ever hear that you guess so. Find another guy if you're going to say stupid shit like that. You know why. Is that why you're here?"

"Yes."

"There, was that so fucking hard? So that's the way I do things. No bullshit. So, to get it out of the way, are you straight?"

"Yes."

"Okay. You have a job where you work with beautiful women, and you like women. You leave that behind. Why the change?"

"Because of what happened to my sister."

"Okay. Do you think that saying only something happened to her would help when sitting here with a fucking therapist!"

"No, but I have a hard time thinking about it. Talking about it will make me think about it."

"That, dear boy, is an honest answer. Let's keep it like that. That I can work with. So, here, we face hard things, so just do it. Tell me what happened to her. Distance yourself if you need to. Make it where you're writing a report about some person if that helps."

"No. I can tell it as now I'm flooded with it since being asked. She went to Morocco after getting her degree in archeology. There was a team there digging based on some finds where they were going to build an airport. I was in the studio when my mother called saying she heard from the dig team she had gone missing. There's a lot about trying to find her, all that. But in the end, she was never found. She still hasn't been found."

"So, there you were with your models and camera, and you're sister goes missing and what? Did you feel guilty you couldn't do anything? Mad at her for going to a dangerous place? Felt helpless to track her?

"Helpless. Yeah. I kept taking pictures and all, and she was taken or dead and I couldn't change what happened."

"Did you do anything about it?"

"I had made a lot of money. I was smart, and I'm pretty strong, you know, athletic. After hearing all kinds of excuses, I canceled all my shoots and got on a plane and go to Morocco. I had been there for a location shoot a year before she was there. I knew it was a mess with all kinds of people there, good and bad. I decided to find her."

"But, you didn't."

"No. A lot went down. I was roughing guys up. I was pretty ruthless. Angry, really. They all acted so fucking dumb, but it was easy to learn what was going on. Pretty young women from here are worth a lot in that part of the world. They abduct them, get them away, sell them. That's what happened to her. I'm sure of it."

"Mike, that's brutal, and I am sorry for your sister. It was good you went and found out what happened. So, at that point, a person can accept it, or keep fighting to find her. So, why go to the agency? How did that happen?"

"I was beating the shit out of one of the guys luring tourist girls. I figured he was part of the group and could give me information. A man, an American, he watched what I was doing, and after I beat the guy unconscious, he came over and asked if I'd like to join the agency. I'd stand a better chance working with them. I talked to him, and he said we had the same mission, but it would be hard on my own. Next thing, I go to DC, go through training, then I'm back to Morocco and working smart. Saved a lot of women, just never my sister."

"You felt that was your calling?"

"Sure. Not before my sister went missing. But at that time. Yes. I was good at it. Really good. I almost didn't get in the agency as I had that anger issue about my sister, but sometimes, that's what they look for. I was that."

"Now, you say you were the best at it. Because you had that anger? You'd do whatever it takes to save anyone going the route of your sister?"

"Exactly."

"See how simple it is? Does saying all that upset you, or frustrate you?"

"Well, neither. I still have that drive to save women in that situation. I still hate people who do that shit to them. I learned my sister was probably alive. She's still of value and they mess them up with drugs or just brainwash them to think they're being taken care of. So, I learned she's most likely alive. I hope to find her — still."

"And that brings us to the question of why you're leaving field work and going intelligence operative in the office. Why?"

"A lot happened. I realized that each group I took down was really a way to find my sister, not to really stop the bigger activities. Then I saw a guy dragging a young girl into a Land Rover. She was all of about 15. I didn't pull her away and interrogate him. I shot him."

"Yeah, you did. And the agency took you off field work and said get therapy or get behind a desk. That's why you're here. But you chose to be behind a desk and get therapy. Are you worried you'd do that again? A guy like that is better off alive to find out who he works for, all that. Is that the reason?"

"No. I'd do it again. That stopped him. I saw that the agency was playing footsie with gathering intelligence. That's why I shot the guy. That did better at saving the girl then endless reports on migrating patterns and suspects. It's not a need to kill, and the agency needed to be sure about that and to prove it, I put me in therapy to find out. I was looking all around when I got back. All the agents sitting at PCs, and they didn't have clue it's real people getting killed or trafficked. That is sick shit. They never shot a fucker grabbing a kid just because he could, because we wouldn't stop him. I just looked and said I could do better than that whole room of guys who didn't know what it was really about. So, I want to change that. Instead of lists of who is doing what, change it to kill lists. It's the only way to stop it. They use fear and terror. I think we'd do better talking their language."

"You told this to the chief at the agency? Just like you did just now?"

"Yes. I said let me, or I quit and start on my own. I think it's where I can do best."

"And he said yes?"

"He said a conditional yes. If I talk to you, and you determine I'm not doing this out of revenge, he'd dedicate a team to it and see how it goes."

Mike recalled that moment. It was Charles who made him figure himself out in that first session. The look on his face. His last question.

"And that's what I'll do. So, just one question. Right from your heart like you've been doing. Are you out for revenge?"

"Absolutely fucking yes."

Charles signed off that he was okay, and had his head on straight. He had to spend more time in therapy as nobody thinks such a truth can be handled in one session. Charles circled back just to be sure, but the reasons remained the same. They talked about photography for two sessions, and explored how getting models to do things was similar to trafficking.

"Yeah, Charles. I see it differently now. Parents groom little girls to look and act like sluts or strippers. Then modeling agencies lure them and snatch them away on assignments. We groom them to be things. Objects. I'll never see it the same now…"

As he pulled into the agency garage, he knew that it was learning that photo auditions were being used for trafficking and pedophilia put it all together in his mind. The traffickers had invaded his domain. Auditions always had a risk of casting calls actually being predators, but this was so blatant and easy for them to do in America. He knew both worlds. He would do something about it, not just compile kill lists for field agents to send messages to the traffickers. He would face the traffickers himself.

Chapter Eighteen
Raising Children Right

Sitting in the room, watching DVDs of American movies on the large screen TV, Angie and Cindy were growing more apprehensive. They were prisoners. They couldn't leave the room and had no idea what would happen to them next. It was torture to sit and worry without an answer. Angie had talked quietly to Cindy about if they could get out somehow, but Cindy knew that would only make things worse. She had a feeling if they did something like that, they would be given to someone who could use force to control them. They were untouched, and they were fed well and given things they had asked for, down to what movies they'd like to watch.

On the third day, the large man came in with a woman who measured them. She appeared to be a seamstress. She was wearing clothes that covered her completely, and all they could see was her eyes.

After she left, Angie asked why she was covered up. Cindy said she guessed she was religious — a muslim, and that's how muslim women dressed. All covered up. The only ones who would see them was their husband — or master if they were a slave. They looked at each other, and both knew that they would be slaves. With the woman measuring them, it would be with some Islamic or Muslim master, not a Russian. It sent chills through them.

Their fear was justified. A day later the large man and cloaked woman returned, and she told them to take all things off. She spoke in English and had a middle eastern accent. The man didn't turn away, and they had no choice. Cindy took her things off first, and the woman put layers of undergarments on her, a burka, then a hijab covering her head and face except for her eyes. The material was red cotton, with white silk embroidery. Next, the woman did the same for Angie, and her garb was all white. They were not given any shoes or sandals. She led them to the mirror, saying they must never take off any of the attire, and never reveal their face except to their master. She spent time showing them how to wind the long scarf-like hijab to be in place perfectly and had them do it over and over until they knew how to do the winding.

Telling them to take off the clothes, she hung them in the closet, saying all fit well and she would be making more for them, and night clothes for bed. Bowing, she turned and left.

Angie stood crying, pointing to the closet. It was certain they would be sent to some rich Arab and be sex slaves, and dressed so, even if anyone came to find them, they would be covered like all the other women in such a place and hard to find. Cindy whispered to Angie, in her ear.

"They are watching us, I'm sure. Let's not fight it right now. Let's take them out and try them on, show we think they are pretty. This is about them trying to get us to be okay with things. Groom us. I keep hearing about that, that young girls are groomed by parents, by society. I'm sure that's what this is all about. So, let's pretend we are."

Walking to the closet, Cindy spoke out loud she thought the clothes were beautiful, and she had always wanted to look so mysterious. She put on the entire outfit, then stared at herself in the mirrors on the closet doors. She twirled around, went and looked in her eyes, rubbed herself all over, saying it was so comfortable and pretty. She told Angie to give it a try, she may like it.

Changing into the new clothes, Angie needed help doing her hijab the first time, but after a second attempt, put it on correctly. She tried sitting, laying on the bed, asking how to drink with your face covered, and she was doing all the right things if their captors were watching.

As they both were in full garb, the door opened, and it wasn't the large man from earlier who entered, but a smaller man, middle-aged, hair slicked back and wearing a perfectly tailored suit. He was heavy, but well groomed, and he seemed familiar to Cindy. She realized he was the man who was talking to Jamie on the stage, and it struck fear in her. He was the man who had bought them.

Following the small man — the trafficker — was a man who was clearly his bodyguard. He was tall, olive complexion, and had a neatly trimmed beard. In a tailored suit, he was handsome but that was not what caught Cindy's attention. She knew him. He was a Ukrainian boy she had played with as a child — the son of one of her father's whores. She looked at him, her head giving the slightest nod, and he did the same. He knew her — and her mother. She realized he most likely saw her on a surveillance video. A surge of hope rushed through Cindy although she showed no such sign for the trafficker to see.

"Ladies, please to sit. We talk. You take nice chairs… Yosh, bring one for me."

As they walked to the stuffed chairs, Yosh reached out in the hallway and carried in a simple padded chair made of wood and put it in front of the eating area. He went back to standing at the door, hands crossed in front of him.

"You have been taken care of. Nicely, yes? Food good? Have what you ask for?"

They were frightened, but managed to nod. They only had their eyes as their face was covered, and he looked right into their eyes.

"I know, I know. Yes, you are scared. Upset. Wonder what happen to me? Here you are, with clothes that cover all from view, but you are wonderful sight, even covered up so. Even more exciting. I am, well, American name, Brian. This my house, you are guests. I have been away, first chance I get to visit. I apologize."

They sat, quiet, and he wanted them to hear him and understand what he was telling them and was going slow.

"I know things many don't. In America, how you live? I hear you in crappy tin box. Poor. Nobody care about you. No go out, no even citizens. True, yes?"

Cindy knew he wanted an answer. She would tell him the truth.

"We weren't citizens but were going to be. No, because of that, we were poor, and we lived in a mobile home, but it was ours. We owned it. We could come and go. We weren't prisoners or kidnapped and drugged…"

"Yes, yes, that is so. Once, I was prisoner. Yes, Brian, prisoner… Like you. I live in box. Crap box called housing. Told what to do, No choice in life. But, Brian, he decides, thinks, why live in crappy box? Why not live like men who run things? So, I meet man, say I don't want to be puppet, you know, one with others pulling strings. Man, he see I mean it. So, he has me go and talk nice to girls. Invite them to fancy place to eat caviar. They eat caviar, then his men take them away. I good at it. Charmer, he say. Suddenly, no more box. No more strings. I have car. I live in nice place. I have money."

Cindy understood too well. She knew exactly what he meant, and she saw no reason to hold back. In full Russian, she told him her story.

"You do that, live like that, but girls become slaves, many killed, maimed. All so you can have house and money. Do you know where I come from? Where I was born?"

Smiling at her reply, he leaned forward, interested in what she was saying. He shrugged, shook his head to say he didn't, and said from her accent, Ukraine perhaps.

"Yes, Ukraine. My father was richer than you. A drug lord. A trafficker. My mother was there at his side. A man like you would work for him. He would treat you like a dog. I was raised thinking drugging young girls and selling them was how to live well. I know all about what you are, what you do. And, if he finds out about where I am, he'll kill you."

With a blank expression, Brian sat back. He put his hand to his chin, thinking. He nodded, then leaned forward to talk.

"Much you say. You say you know what I do. You say come from same life. Why, in America, live like whore? In metal box? No money? I am curious. Please, to tell me… Why you live like dirt?"

"First off, we don't live like dirt. You insult me and my daughter."

Putting his hands up, Brian shook his head over and over.

"I make judgment. I no think. Know not why. That is why I ask, so please, to forgive me. I ask right. Why to live such way?"

"You haven't apologized for what you said of us. You apologized for making a judgment when you know nothing about us."

"You are truly drug czar daughter. No afraid. But, you, yes, correct. Please, I sorry.. I know nothing, and insult you."

"That is what a man says. I ask you, now. Are you a man, or a low down pimp my father would piss on?"

Fire showed in his eyes. She had hit him where it hurt as she knew that's all he was down deep inside. He looked like he wanted to lash out, but contained himself.

"Cindy, that is name, yes? Good. I wish to be respected man. Hard when, in life, you start off as low down pimp as you say. But, I am no more that. I could still be, but no, I am better than that. So, let us not judge each other… yet. Tell me of why you no here, but in bad place in horrible America."

"That is simple. When a man gets power, he can use it to do good things, or he can use it to be a powerful monster. My father used drugs, fucked his whores, had no respect for anyone including me. He fucked me, and when I was a little girl, 12, got me pregnant. My mother is a ruthless bitch, and she got me out because if he found out I was pregnant, he would have let me have my child, then sell her. My mother killed a lot of people in her way when getting me out. She was on a rampage. If she hears about me, I know she'll kill you. You won't see it coming. She'll act like a slut, get to you and blow your brains out. I watched her do it many times. She told me to lay low in America, and forget her and my father…"

He stared at her, and so did Angie. He sat, wordless, looking at her. She let him know there was more than just her mother to deal with.

"But, big real man Brian. I haven't forgotten one fucking thing I learned from them on how to treat lowlife scum pimps. Kill me now or I sure as hell will kill you."

She saw his eyes. He showed fear. He was taking what she said seriously, and didn't know what to do. After looking at her, her eyes into his, for near five minutes, he finally spoke.

"You… Yes, mean what you say. I no think you could do, but mean it. Who is father?"

"Do you think for one minute I would tell you? Again, you insult me. Apologize for treating me like some fucking girl on drugs in that shit apartment where you came from."

Cindy was shocked, and shaking in terror as how could her mother talk like that and not be killed. Her too. Brian sat, stunned as she was. He shrugged again.

"You right. Again, mistake to talk such way. I apologize. I thought… If I knew him… We could…"

"Stop. Now. That's a fucking excuse. No reason. No excuse. You insult me. You hold me. I know the deal. You sell us off to some arrogant sheik, think it's all over. No, motherfucker. It won't be. I'll fucking kill him after I bite his dick off, then hunt you down and I'll shove his pathetic dick in your mouth, then watch you eat it and swallow it. If you take too long, I'll shoot you in your smarmy mouth and that will get it in you."

He stood up, but paused, looking back at Yosh, then sat back down. He was confused and he was in a bind. Cindy was sure he had already taken the money for them. He would be killed if he harmed them — or messed the sale up. At the same time, he saw how she could be tame as a lamb or the Ukrainian drug czar bitch she was revealing. She didn't wait for him to say anything.

"You're fucked. You know it. You fuck this deal up, you're dead. There's a long line of fuckers as pathetic as you to take your place. You hand us to him, even with a warning, we act all afraid like we have been. We say you raped us and we are so glad he saved us. He will know you did. He will think you're a pussy for warning him with such a stupid story. I wait it out, and I off him, cut off his dick, then show up before you hear he's dead and feed it to you. You pathetic dickless creep. What are you going to do? Kill us? Then he'll kill you. One of his many henchmen will. He will make a show of it, like with Vlad at your joke of an auction. He'll eat fig leaves as he watches. Maybe your boy there works for him. How can you be sure? If you're so fucking smart, figure out a different option. What's the third option where you at least live to fuck up another day?"

She looked past him to Yosh who was watching carefully.

"Yosh. Shoot this fucker now and I'll call my mom and you can take over this operation."

Cindy nodded at Yosh. The intensity in his manner and body language. In his eyes. They flashed. He was already persuaded. Most men in his position hated being treated like nothing and thought they could do a better job than the man they worked for.

Brian turned to Yosh, screaming at him to leave the room.

Yosh didn't move.

For the first time, Yosh spoke.

"I born in Ukraine. Know her mother. I was born to one of their whores."

Brian stared at him, and saw him take out an Uzi from under his suit coat. He turned back to Cindy.

"New plan! New plan! I let you be partner, live like queen. No more live in fear in America. Here. Rich. Take care daughter right!"

He was shaking. Sweating. Cindy was cold as ice, and Angie was in a state of shock. She had no idea her mother could be so powerful. She knew she had the man frightened and anything could happen.

"No. You drugged us. Let other sick fucks stick fucking filthy fingers in my daughter's ass. Put us in this prison to hold until your sheik boy comes to get us. I wouldn't shit on you, let alone believe your fucking lies."

She looked to Yosh.

"I know my mother's number. I'll call her. Tell her what happened and you saved us. You know she's fucking ruthless, but for that, she will reward you. She'll have people here come and clean things up, and I'll tell her to let you run this shitshow like a real Ukrainian."

As she spoke, Yosh was keeping his eyes on Brian. Cindy instantly learned why.

Brian jumped up and pulled a pistol from his shoulder holster and started to aim it at her. As soon as he pulled out the gun, an explosive barrage of bullets fired from Yosh's Uzi and Brian went flying. He landed face up in the corner of the room, at least a dozen holes oozing blood.

Hearing shouts and sounds of men running towards the room, Yosh ran to the hall, then Cindy and Angie heard a number of rounds being fired. Yosh was shooting the other guards and lackeys as she and Cindy were changing into regular clothes. When the shooting stopped, they both turned and saw Yosh standing in the doorway, the Uzi no longer in his hand. He was nodding. Cindy smiled at him.

"Thank you, Yosh. I appreciate what you did. We need to finish changing, then I'd like to call Eliana."

Nodding, smiling at her, he turned and left the room, giving them privacy. Angie stood, still in a state of shock, looking at Cindy.

"Mom… What? How did you do that?"

Cindy held up her hand to indicate she'd answer in a moment, Angie knowing that sign. Cindy went to Brian's bullet-riddled body and spat into what remained of his face, just as her mother did after shooting her father. She reached to his hand, took his pistol, a Glock, looked at it, then smiled at Angie as she stood up and told Angie it would be nice to sit and has some pastries and water.

Still in awe, Angie managed a smiled, heading to the table still filled with snacks. Cindy took a kolachki, Angie taking one as well, and she sighed after drinking some water, still holding the pistol. Angie looked at her, waiting. Cindy made a sigh, then was ready to talk.

"See this stupid thing? It does nothing until someone decides to use it. The little bullets in it? If used on us, we'd both be dead. Dead. I didn't need this thing to stop that man. I stopped him by not being afraid of him. But, there won't always be a Yosh standing by to use one of these for us. From now on, neither of us will ever be without a gun like this on us. It's the only thing most men understand. Brian sure did…"

Angie looked at her, listening intently. She looked at the gun, held out her hand and Cindy gave it to her. She started weighing it using one hand, examining it, then raising her leg straight up, put the Glock to her upper thigh, smiling. She looked up at Cindy.

"Mom, I think if we get thigh holsters we could carry two of them and nobody will know we have them on."

Handing the gun back to Cindy, she smiled at Angie, impressed at how smart she always was. Lifting her long leg up while reclining in the chair, she put the Glock against her bare thigh, nodding at it, then Angie.

"Perfect. I hope they make frilly holsters. We'll have Yosh give us more guns and use some stocking tops to hold them for now."

Angie got up, went to the closet and got their stay-up nylons with the wide elastic top. Handing a pair to Cindy, she sat down and clutched hers as she spoke.

""Mom, I tried on so many of yours growing up. They should do for now, and we have all your sexy ones at home… But, mom! How did you know how to do all of that? Geez! I've never herd you swear before, even.."

Smiling at her with all her love, Cindy understood Angie's surprise.

"I grew up watching my father and mother do this kind of thing. I hated it. It was everything I vowed not to be… and for you to never have to be. But, here? Today? I realized it was the only way out. Angie. This is real important. I meant what I said to Brian. What I would do. I live with what I saw my mom do to my father. It's a part of me. Not the only part of me, like with them… But, it's part of who I am. I want you to know that. I will always tell you the truth. And, sweetie… The truth is I want you to be as strong as I was today. In this world, for a girl as beautiful as you… It's be taken… "

Cindy slid the chamber of the gun back, letting the bullet fly out into her hand. She held it up for Angie to see.

"Taken… or not taken. This will be how you will be not taken — ever again."

Angie held out her hand. Cindy put the bullet in her waiting palm.

"Mom. We need lots of these. And clutches to carry tons of them. But, mom… How did you know Yosh after all those years? Oops! Sorry! I mean as you are all both all grown up now."

Cindy about melted hearing Angie take back the how many years reference, but knew it was not implying she was old. She wasn't, and understood her saying it that way.

"Yosh? I can spot a Ukrainian, no problem. But he still looks a lot like when he was 12. I recognized him, and he gave me a little nod he knew it was me when he walked in. I knew he was the son of one of my dad's girls who had gotten older and did housework for us, and that sure helped. I've always made sure to remember my mom's number. I'm going to do what I promised."

As she finished explaining how she knew him, there was a knock on the door, then it slowly opened as Yosh stood waiting in the doorway. Cindy smiled at him, saying no need to be shy and they were dressed, so please join them for some kolachki. His face lit up as he took the chair he had brought in for Brian then sat with them as Cindy handed him a plate with a smile. He ate one, his eyes closing, clearly enjoying the treat.

"This just like mother made for me. You, and Janoush too. It is like being little, in your yard. Cynthia, what of brother? Is he with you in trailer?"

Angie realized Yosh had been friends with her uncle, Jakey. She was ready to cry. So much bad had happened because of trafficking. She could only be sad as Cindy explained to Josh what happened, his face showing sadness near as great as hers.

"Cindy, that is a sadness I will now carry. We were friends. Sorry, I am, to remind you of such sorrow. This life… Not good one. This will make me think about what I am. But I happy it be me here this day. I am happy you strong, like Eliana. But, I no think you trafficker like her. You always kind person. Not like her that way."

"Yosh, you can do right. You can do good. I hope you save girls, not take them. That will give you a smile, not sadness. I know the boy I grew up with. What your mother wanted you to be. Yosh. Be that. I did what had to be done today. You did what had to be done. You saved our lives. Ahead, save lives. Be a man, not a coward like Brian."

Looking at her, he said he had much to think about.

"Cynthia? Right now. Saying to come. Have pastry with you? First kind thing given me since my mother died."

He held up another kolachki, looked at it, then Cindy.

"This, I will think of each day. Let it guide me. It brought me to this table. Hear faith you have, in me. Only flour and lard, some

                                        Innocence Taken

apricot. Stronger than gun. Thank you. For kolachki…"

He ate it, nodded, then explained that all was clear, asking what she wanted to do. In perfect Ukrainian, she answered.

"What I said I would. I'm going to call my mother, and get you fixed up and safe. I'll tell her to make it where all know it was an attack from a rival, and you were away and came back to this mess. It will take a little time. Where is a phone, and we want out of this room.

Smiling, he nodded, then said follow him. They walked over dead bodies, and soon they learned it was just a house. A large mansion, but just a house. She asked if there were more men who would show up, and he said no, they were all there and didn't expect him to fire. Leading them to the plush living room, he said the landline was secure, and he would leave them for some privacy, but asked if they were hungry. They both nodded, and he said he would make lunch for them all.

Angie listened to Cindy talk to her mother. She said it was a safe line, and they were both outside of Moscow, then explained all that had happened. She heard her deal with her promise toward the end of the call.

"No, absolutely not. I made a deal, and it has to be honored. He saved us, and he's one of your girl's son. You do right by him. I need you to send some men to clean things up here. There's a lot of bodies to get rid of. Bring Glocks for us, too. At least four… No, I don't care about what happened after you fled;. I'm just glad you're okay. When you come, you will finally meet Angie… Yes, I named her Angel. We both look like you… Okay, how long? A local team to clean up? Then a day or so for you? Okay, we have plenty here, and I don't think anyone will be surprised at the gunplay. I know, it's been horrible. I have more to do… Oh, I made another promise. I'll tell you when you get here. Bye, and Angie is waving bye too."

Chapter Nineteen
Oh, It's Trauma Time Again

After the jet had taken off, Jamie sat looking at Mike. Everything had happened so fast, and he had turned everything around. More surprising, he seemed to understand the world she came from. On the ride to the airstrip, and in the car, she was afraid she was being handed off or set up, but she had time to think about what she had been told and wanted to be sure.

"Mike, how could you trust me after what I've been? I'm worried you're going to hand me off to that bastard to get back at me."

It was the first thing she had said to him since getting in the car, and he understood her fear. He knew she would ask and worry that was the situation.

"Jamie, sure, I'd be thinking that too. And, how can you believe an agent like me who goes deep undercover and was almost about to do some minors, right?"

She nodded.

"Well, you can believe or not believe. Look, here's the truth — and the reason. I was a for-real glamour photographer. Great family, doing well. Then, my only sister went to do archeology in Morocco. She was beautiful, young, right out of college, and one day she was gone. Taken. Trafficked. I went and did everything I could to find her, but on my own? I didn't make a dent. An agent saw me, watched me, and said join up where I could at least stop the large traffickers. So, I stopped my photography, and joined. Turned out I was really good at it. It's all about my sister, I won't shit you. I still dream I'll find her one day. I saw Angie and Cindy in the paper, and it just struck a thing in me. It was like how I felt about my sister being taken all over again. So, I went to save them if I could, and found you."

She sat, listening, and she understood. He was good at what he did. He had taken her down. She didn't understand how he knew about her past. That wasn't in any records, at least that she knew about.

"That makes sense, but I have a question. I'm guilty of a lot of things, I know. But your guy who questioned me came and said you wanted me with on this deal. That you knew I was trapped in what I was doing because I had been trafficked. How could you possibly know that?"

Mike looked at her, and she had a desperation in her expression. She wanted to know that someone understood.

"Jamie, I pulled so many kids and women out from captors, and they all have a look. An attitude. Hiding what happened because they're ashamed. Think it's their fault for just being pretty or young. You know it all. Grooming them to be that. Well, you have that look. I can tell, but I don't think anyone else could. I also know that for some, to fucking just get treated like human beings, they're offered that if they recruit for their trafficker. I saw that's what you were doing. It was that, or… well, probably killed if not. I saw that… felt that… well, I just did."

She started to tear up, and she just stared at him. Her eyes were large, and she looked completely different than when he first met her. He knew it wasn't an act.

"Was it when we were… you know, on the table?"

He nodded, giving her a soft smile.

"Yes. That wasn't just sex. It was you craving affection. You know… let me see if I can explain it. Well, for me, being in a woman is the only time I can be sure of what she's about. It just is so clear. You wanted to make love. Be loved. Am I wrong?"

She pushed her shoulders in, her hands between her legs, and tilted her head as she looked up at him.

"No. You had it right."

He waited, watching her life of being used melt away, at least with him. She was a victim, and like so many victims who are groomed, did whatever they needed to do to stay alive by pleasing their masters.

"I was sure of it. I wanted to give you a chance to free yourself. And that's what we're going to do. Your master, Brian or whatever his Russian name is, we're going to kill him. And, free Angie and Cindy. Are you with me?"

Nodding her head while looking him in the eyes, she sighed.

"Yes. I know you can't trust me with a gun, but if I had one, I'd kill him."

Then, she broke down, sobbing. He saw all her pain pouring out. He knew she was thinking of all the girls she had sent off to traffickers under the influence of Brian. As she gathered herself, he leaned over and took both of her hands. She looked into his eyes.

"Mike… I took all those girls and ruined their lives. Young, trusting girls… and that's not all. The guy I hired you to replace? He was fucking killing some to get off. Killing someone! To fucking cum! I shot him in his fucking sick head. I had to wait it out. He knew the whole operation and it was me or him. But those girls… dead… and I let it happen!"

Mike saw she had emotionally isolated herself from what she had done to survive. It was horrific, but that was what the sick need for trafficked children did to everyone involved. All those lives ruined so some rich fuck could have the power of having a child to own and do what they wanted with. How many of those ended up in dumpsters or chippers or were tortured or things even worse that only those doing such things could imagine. She was right. She had done all of that. She was a victim the same as the newest trafficked child. She found a way to survive, and the questions were if she was aware that it was where she could have walked into the building he worked in, told his agency what happened, and said she didn't want to be a victim any longer and wanted to turn people in. He needed to know and explained that to her. She sat, listening, and he saw she was feeling guilty on top of her personal trauma. She either faced it or faced a life in prison. He asked her to simply tell him if she had ever thought of stopping what she was doing by turning Brian over.

She sat, staring ahead. She slowly began shaking her head. She started to cry again but stopped herself and replied.

"No. I never thought to do that. I won't make an excuse about it. Brian, those men, part of what they do is tell someone like me they have their guys in your department. And I wouldn't be surprised if they did. From the start, any thought of turning him in meant I'd be killed. I made a choice. I'm going to face what I did. I'd never pass a polygraph saying I wanted to do anything like that. Sucks, doesn't it? The whole fucking thing. It sucks. I'm sorry, Mike. I told you the truth. It sucks too."

He was watching her and for all her matter-of-factness, he could tell she was facing a truth where she was putting herself in the same league as the men who trafficked, but he knew that wasn't so. She was groomed, brainwashed, and lived in endless fear. The traffickers would kill anyone who posed a threat to them. He knew he could let her continue to feel guilty for crimes done to her mind or see if she was at a point if she could face the truth and redeem herself. He looked at her and didn't show any judgment.

"This is what I think I can do. I'll call in a short while to see if it will play well. We do this. Take him down, get Angie and Cindy, and then we go back. Now, I mean everything I'm going to say.

When that happens, before this jet heads back, if you want, walk away. You'll be in Russia, and you won't face charges there, and you know the other traffickers. That's one option. The second one, well, like I said, I need an authorization, but what I would offer is we all go back, and once there, yeah, you'll still be under arrest, but I think we can turn all that bad done to you into something good. First, we have your laptop, all the names, dates, etc. If you turn on them, work with us to get them all with what you know that would never be put on a laptop, that would have you working with us, not against us. That isn't quite enough to get you off completely. But, as you will swear to what happened to you, how you were under fear of death, traumatized, groomed since a kid, if you agree to get help, some fucking hard-ass therapy, once the shrink says you are right, I think then you can have charges dropped. I'd only do that if you convince me, here, now, that you'll join us to fight this shit. Do you understand what I just said?"

"Yes, yes. I understand. If you can believe me, I want to get those fuckers. The shit they had me doing, they should all have their fucking nuts, then heads, shot off. And I want to be okay, not afraid. But what shrink would ever say I was okay, over all that?"

Smiling, Mike said he knew a good shrink. He wondered how many days it would take Charles to get her righted. He was sure it wouldn't take long. She'd never forget, but he would help her understand that she was no longer a victim, and she could make a choice of what to do with her life.

"I have a guy… Not like you'd thing a shrink is like. My guess is my guy will help you. He helped me. So, I was full of hate and rage. Here I am, with a trafficker, and I'm able to understand that bad things make more bad things happen, and it has to stop. So, am I full of hate and rage right now?"

Finally smiling at him, she told him no. He was amazing.

"Okay, I'm going to open up to you. Fuck yeah, I'm full of hate and rage. That's in me. A trauma, just like yours. But I found a way to do some good with it. And now? I'm not full of hate and rage at you, or just people. It's there for the fuckers who did that to you and everyone else they serve. Without it, how could I do this? This isn't some video game. It's life and death. I'm in all the way. I just want you to know what drives me, and my shrink is the one who helped me put my trauma in the right place. I truly hope he will do that for you. That is the only way to get back at those fuckers. To stop them controlling you and feeling it's your fault. It has to happen or stay in Russia if that's your thing. I need to know. You get off this plane and walk away if you're one of them, or you face Brian and show him he can't do a fucking thing to you ever again. That he's done. That's where it's at."

She was looking at him, her eyes admiring him, looking at him the way she did when they fucked. She was going with her feelings, not her grooming.

"I'm not going to walk away."

Looking at her, that was all he needed to hear.

"I'm going to use some of our flight time to tell James, the guy you dealt with, all I told you. He will be the one to make the deal. No promises yet, but even some of that would be great, okay?"

Nodding, smiling at him, she showed affection and appreciation, and he was surprised at what he was doing. What Charles had told him in therapy had come true. He was right in his mind, and doing right.

After his call, he came and sat across from her.

"James said he was pretty sure, if the shrink helps you like he did me, that he can put the deal on the table for you. And… oh hell, he keeps razzing me because our agent saw us going at each other, and he says of course, I'm all hot for you and lovey-dovey."

She laughed, not sarcastically, in an understanding way. She leaned over, smiling at him with a shy look on her face.

"Well, aren't you? I am…"

He recalled Charles saying no bullshit, just say what it is. It was excellent advice.

"Yes. I am. But our secret for now, okay? After that, I want to wail on you. There. That's what I learned from the shrink. To express my true feelings. Isn't it great?"

Chapter Twenty
Soft Landing

On their landing approach, Mike got a call from James saying their assets had surveyed Brian's house, and they were fully sure he had been put down. Mike was shocked at the news, but not as much as learning that Cindy had taken over and she just had a visit from a woman with her own jet. She was identified as a major trafficker in the Ukraine, and the most powerful one in all of Eastern Europe. The noise on the ground was that it was Cindy's mother.

"James, I'm floored. I hope this wasn't all a setup. My gut tells me it wasn't. Jamie would have been hit or part of it if her mother had set it up with Brian. My guess is she found a way to get in touch with her mother, and that solved being taken. Well, even with that, we're there to take Cindy and Angie home, and find out all we can. So, you're sure about Brian? Okay… I'll think it through… Well, assuming it's her mother, they'll freak seeing Jamie… Right, good advice. I'll go in first and explain things… Okay, once done, I'll report."

Listening to him, Jamie was sitting, mouth opened, stunned.

"My God! Cindy? She took over? And what's that about her mother? A trafficker with her own jet? Oh, yeah, they see me, they'll wail on me, but not the way you want to!"

Seeing Jamie fully in a new light, he thought she had the last part right. She looked like one of the girls she had taken. Shocked.

"You'll be okay. I'll go in myself. They don't know me. Hopefully they'll accept I'm a fed there to rescue them. You know what? Stay in the jet. I'll tell the truth. Brian had you doing the recruiting, or he'd kill you. How you turned against Brian and were working with us to save them. If needed, I'll call Yorgi, their lawyer friend, and he'll verify it. Maybe I'll do that first. The guy is worried sick about them. Then, if it's safe, I'll send the car for you."

As the jet landed, once it pulled into a hanger there was a long limo waiting for them. He unlocked a case he had stowed away, taking out a Glock special and holster, putting it under his arm. He said he'd get things straightened out while she stayed in the jet. Running from the jet to the limo, she called his name. Telling the driver to stop, he opened the car door and she reached in and gave him a gentle kiss. Smiling, he said that was a nice start.

Talking to the driver, he said Brian's place was close to the airport, which made sense as transporting girls involved flights, and holding them until sold. Amazed at how the area looked much like any affluent suburb in America, it wasn't what most people would imagine when thinking of Russia. In less than fifteen minutes, the driver pulled into a long driveway and said as they weren't expected, be prepared to be questioned and searched. Mike said he expected that, and appreciated the warning.

Pulling up to the main entry door, Mike got out of the backseat. Holding his hands up, one of them with his federal ID, Yosh was standing in front of the large door, holding his Uzi, not showing any emotion and as Mike reached the first step, he told him to stop, keep his hands up and explain why he was there.

"Hello. My name if Mike, and I'm a CIA agent. I am here to learn the status of two women who were taken from the US. I am certain they were brought here. I am hoping they are alive, and I wish to help them. Their names are Cindy and Angie, a mother and her daughter. I will tell you if needed I was going to force the issue and retire Brian if needed for taking US citizens. I am only interested in taking the two women back to their home. Agents here tell me Brian has already been stopped. Is that correct?"

Nodding, Yosh said he'd need more than that. Mike understood.

"Well, I can provide proof of who I am, and what I told you is

                    Innocence Taken

true. I'm going to lower one hand to take out my phone. I know you are pointing your gun and if I do anything other than take out my phone you will stop me. Once I have my phone, I'm going to call Cindy's trusted friend, Yorgi, her lawyer. Please listen to the call as I will put it on speaker. I'm going to explain I was sent to rescue her and her daughter, but as she has never met me, and he has, he can explain to her who I am, and that I'm a friend. I'm going to set my phone down on the wall once I get him and talk to him. I will tell him to stay on the phone so he may talk to Cindy. Then, I'll back away. I ask that you get it, then give it to Cindy. Is that okay with you? She will know instantly who Yorgi is, and she will wish to speak with him."

Getting a nod, he made the call, and Yorgi was ecstatic hearing the news. He told him he needed to explain to Cindy who he was, that he was there to rescue her, and help her understand he was there to take her home. He said it would take a few minutes to get her on the phone, and he said he'd wait.

Putting the phone on the top of a low wall surrounding the house, Yosh kept an eye on him and took the phone, then backed up into the house with his Uzi pointed at Mike as he shut the door once in the house. Mike waited close to ten minutes, then Yosh appeared in the doorway, saying, "Friend, please to come in."

Once in the house, there stood Cindy and Angie, two people he had only seen pictures of, and they were smiling as Angie went and hugged him. A woman, looking only a bit older than Cindy but beautiful, clearly related as they all looked alike, was standing behind them. She was in expensive clothes, nodding at all that was going on. After Angie let him go, Cindy came and hugged him just as hard.

"Mike, Yorgi told us how you were risking it all to come save us. Thank you, Mike! Oh, thank you. I can't believe it. And he said you wanted to take the leader, that Brian, down as well. Oh! I was so excited I didn't introduce you to my mother. She lives in the

Ukraine. Mike, Yorgi said you're a smart man, and a good man. There's something you should know…"

Jumping in between Mike and Eliana, Angie was holding out her arms to protect Cindy's mother.

"Please, promise me you won't arrest her!"

Taking one of Angie's hands, Cindy gave her a serious look, telling her to let them meet each other, and all would be explained, but being respectful comes first.

Reaching out, he shook Eliana's hand, and she nodded at him.

"I think my daughter learned too well. Learned from me. Maybe, runs in family, but I hope not. Good girl. Such wonderful granddaughter she give me. Well, Yosh, he will tell you things that happen. How Brian took my girls. Yosh, he knew Brian was shit. Took care of things after call from me. He will help clean things up. I glad you here, take girls home safe. I have enemies here, so must to go. Give me moment with girls."

He walked away with Yosh, who filled him in on the whole series of events. Mike was astonished. Maybe the mother was right. She had learned a lot growing up, but he knew that's not who she was, it was what she needed to do to survive. He kept thinking of all the people he knew who needed to do things to just survive. It made him shiver.

Just as the story was fully explained, Angie was following behind Cindy as she walked out with her mother, hugging her as she got in her limo and stood watching it drive away.

Walking back into the house, Mike stood looking in awe of Cindy. They each started to say there was more to talk about. They laughed, and Cindy said for him to go first. He explained, in detail, about Jamie and how, like them, she was trafficked and forced into doing what Brian had commanded to do or kill her. He said she took a huge risk and was there to rescue them and apologize. He asked if they could understand she was like them, now free from her sick master. Cindy and Angie looked at each other, and they said as he had faith in her, they would too. If she had been through what they had, they could understand. Mike called the driver and told him to bring Jamie to the house.

Once Jamie arrived, they were all a bit apprehensive and cautious, but then Cindy, elated that she had come to do right, went and hugged her, saying enough of that stuff. Mike watched fears on all of them slip away, and they were all united. He asked Cindy what she wished to talk about.

"Well, I know Yosh told you what I promised I would do to the man we were being sold to. I meant it then and mean it more now. I am going to kill him."

Mike looked at her, and knew she couldn't have been more serious. He understood. Even more, he wanted to kill the man and stop him buying women, then use him to warn as many others as he could.

"Yosh, were you bringing them there, or was he coming here?"

"Here, he will come. Get them, look other girls over as gifts for his men. Tomorrow, he comes."

Mike thanked him, then turned to the three women.

"Well, I don't know about you, but I could use a night out on the town in Moscow. Nice dinner, dancing, get some dresses you like. Sound good?

Chapter Twenty One
A Prince and Paupers

After a nice night, knowing both Cindy and Angie only had dresses covering them head to toe as if they were shopping in the middle east, they had started the evening by going to boutiques that had the latest in fashions. Mike, having permission to use as much as was needed on the mission, told them to go wild and get lots of outfits. The smiles on their faces was worth the whole experience. They explained they only shopped at thrift stores, and it was really their first-time finding clothes that were new, and just for them.

Smiling as they tried everything they could find in double zeros, he was happy the prices were all in rupees as they would have fainted if they knew how much they cost. Telling them each to find at least ten full outfits, they were a wonder to watch. As a glamour photographer, he was stunned at how everything they put on had them looking as if featured in one of his most famous fashion shoots. After somehow deciding on only ten full outfits, putting on their favorite pick in a dressing room when finished, he watched them throw their middle eastern sheaths in a trash can.

They looked happy. The way they could have all their life if they hadn't been hiding from the world of trafficking Cindy came from. Faces filled with smiles, laughing, twirling to see how their clothes moved, their joy was stunning, and it was the first time in years he wished he had his camera with him.

While they were trying on most everything in each store, he and Jamie went walking, her arm in his, and he told her about his life growing up, how it had changed, and now was changing again. She told him about her life before being abducted, and he didn't ask her to talk about that part as it would be painful. He would learn in time. She hadn't had a family like his, and grew up with a sad woman who was a hooker working truck stops for a pimp in the Mojave desert. Knowing it was too soon to ask more, he said that was something he would want to understand when she was ready to talk about it. To make some light shine in that dark, he said even in such a circumstance when she was little, what had she wanted to be when she grew up. Knowing there may not be an answer, it was a risky question, but she smiled at it.

"You are not going to believe it. I mean, really. You're not going to believe it. I wanted to be a fashion model."

He left it there, but it made sense. She had a natural sway in her walk, a certain way of standing, a way of looking at him that spelled out style and grace. She had a calm nature, even after all she had been through. He knew she was still mired in the world she had been in, but all people think about life ahead. Asking her now that things had changed, were there any dreams she may have now.

"Well, Mike… Gee. Well, first I need to find some really good guy who'll treat me nice and let me be nice to him. Then, lots and lots of loving all the time. I'd want being together to make us feel happy, special. I'd show how much I love him. Hear him say how much he loves me, and not have to say it as I'd know he did. And… Anything else? Job? Anything good, helping people. The job would fall in place if I had all the important things."

He watched her look at him the whole time she said it all. It was something he would always treasure, and he wished Charles was there as she had just come right out and said who and what she was inside.

"Well, good luck with finding a great guy like that!"

Stopping, standing looking at each other in front of the store where Cindy and Angie were finishing up, they looked at each other and held hands. Looking up into his eyes, she said it would certainly be the first time she'd have something good happen in her life, but she had a good feeling about it. Telling her he felt the same way, they kissed and held each other as people walked past, then heard Angie call to them as she and Cindy came walking out of the store.

"Mike, innocent eyes!"

Knowing she had just been taken, sold to a billionaire, seen a man shot, she was just as she said. A sweet young girl, and she still had her innocence.

Carrying vast quantities of clothes in bags, Mike led them to a place impossible to get in, but with a call to headquarters, suddenly there was the best table in the house ready for them. Being a top agent had some benefits, one of them being meetings at unexpected places like a trendy eatery. He had called a bit earlier to learn which one would be the best, but he let on as if he hadn't called.

After caviar that was impossible to get anywhere else, and a sampling menu of things that they didn't know could be eaten, he watched how Cindy and Angie looked at him, each look was one of thanks and admiration. He sensed that Cindy was a bit disappointed he was clearly taken with Jamie, and he realized she would be a wonderful catch for a good man. His look told her that, and they seemed to have an understanding. He liked Cindy and Angie and admired that they could smile after all they had been through, and most of all be kind to Jamie. He wondered if he could be as nice to one who had taken his sister. He left that one alone. It was a night to forget horrible events, not to remember.

The next morning, after a light breakfast, Cindy made it clear what she wanted to have happen. It worried Mike, and it was brutal to even think about. Asking if Angie would be there, she nodded, slowly, saying, "Of course."

They had gotten free because her mother had done much the same thing to save her, and she had watched. It was how she was able to stand up to Brian. She said no man would ever do anything to harm Angie again, and she wanted her there with her.

"Mike. Think about what is really going on. There's a man who plans to make her his slave. Make me his slave too. He'll be taught that's not something a person does to anyone. I want Angie to see how to treat any man who thinks that, or dare do it."

Realizing Cindy was not running from such a nightmare, she was taking control of what would happen. Stopping the man, Angie by her side, was just as much for Angie as for Cindy's own disgust and to make sure she'd be the one to stop him. No government, agency, or any other person. She would do what all others weren't doing. She would stop him from ever doing such a thing to another person forever.

Jamie whispered to Mike to let it happen. They needed closure. Just like she wanted to kill Brian, although she didn't. Leaning in closer, she said she had him, but Cindy and Angie had nobody except each other. Then she told him something that would stay with him, change him, forever.

"I wish my mother had done that for me."

Mike looked at her, and it was as if he had taken a bullet. One of truth. The women trafficked hadn't been protected. Cindy was doing what all loves or parents needed to do. Stop traffickers before they took the ones they loved.

Yosh had been listening to the plan, and was a part of it. The house phone rang, and he went to answer it, then coming back saying the sheik's jet had just landed. Mike started to get up, but Yosh told him it would be about an hour as they had to unload the custom Rolls Royce that he took everywhere. Mike shook his head, wishing he would be the one taking him down.

Nodding, Cindy and Angie got up, saying they were going to get dressed and stay in the room they had been in. Jamie said she be in

Brian's bedroom as she would be questioned about why she was there.

Mike was going to act as a guard and not say anything even though his Russian was excellent. He would play the muscle who didn't take notice of what was going on. Yosh would explain that Brian had gone to bring the other girls from where they were kept, and he'd escort him to inspect his purchase. With that, the door to the prison room was shut, Yosh and Mike standing outside, each on one side of the front door.

Waiting a short time, they saw the bright white Rolls Royce driving to the house, and they remained still. As it pulled up to the front of the house, Mike watched as the driver got out and opened the door. There was only the driver and the sheik, no guards. The man was so confident he didn't feel the need for anyone to protect him, and he didn't want any of his men to see his purchases as they were for his eyes alone.

As the sheik got out of the back of the car, Mike was surprised. He was a young man, perhaps twenty. Tall, thin, good looking, he was handsome and had a perfectly trimmed beard, wearing a white sheath and traditional head covering with bands around his head. Smiling, thanking his driver, the man got back in the car. Calmly walking up the few stairs to the front door, he bowed with a traditional welcome gesture, and spoke in Russian. Yosh, welcoming him with respect, explained he was to show him to his purchase, saying Brian was still out picking the finest girls for his men's pleasure and would be back soon. He gestured to him to go in, following him while Mike remained guarding the front door.

Waiting, taking longer than he expected, he heard shots fired. The driver had the windows down, and hearing the shots pulled an automatic rifle from the front floor and threw open the driver-side door to get out of the car. Waiting for such an action, Mike had his Glock out and shot at him while still in the car.

Flying from shots to his head, the driver flew out of the car as

Mike fired even as he flew. He went to him, firing into his head, taking no chances. Yosh rushed out of the door, Uzi at the ready, but Mike waved all was okay as he headed into the house.

Once inside, he saw Jamie in the hall, looking into the prison room, then going in. Knowing the sheik was dead as Jamie showed no caution entering, she came back out holding Cindy and Angie's hands, leading them to the living room. Although she'd been in the room next to them, she hadn't seen what happened. After sitting, Cindy patted Angie's leg, asking her if she was okay. Angie nodded, saying it was awesome. Mike knew she had witnessed a brutal killing, also knowing it was the only way they would ever be free. Cindy looked at Jamie, who nodded in understanding, then to Mike.

"It went just like we planned. A bit better, in a way, if such a thing can be good or better. We were standing there, all timid like you suggested. We had our hands behind our backs, our heads down to only look at him when he said to. I had the pistol in the pouch on the back of my burka we sewed in last night in case he wanted to hold or see my hands. He went to Angie first and pulled her face veil off. He looked at her, no expression. Then he went to me and did the same thing. He gave a little nod. Then, he did things different than we expected…"

She looked at Angie, and she nodded at her for being brave during it all, and patted her hands. Cindy looked back to tell what happened next.

"He knelt down. Right in front of me. I was shocked. He was young. I only had the burka on, nothing else. He knelt there, then lifted it up. All the way high, to see my mound. I saw his head nodding in approval… That really was a tough moment… Him nodding at me… Judging me like that. It took all I had to stand there and not react. Then, never looking up at me, he moved his face in and stuck his tongue in my slit, then started to go at me, you know, his tongue moving up and down, in and out. He was moaning with pleasure…"

She stopped for a moment, shaking her head. It was just to get ready for the next part.

"Well, seeing him so happy doing that, so preoccupied with me, I gently moved my hand from behind me with the gun ready, safety off. I slowly moved it to be in front of me, and I had moved it about six inches above his head, and then, I gently pulled the trigger. Like you showed me. Point down, straight into the middle of the top of his head. But, even though that close, one shot would kill him, I fired four rounds nonstop. His head exploded. It was just like a water balloon. With the burka up, my legs were splattered, my feet, and well, my whole lower half. He was dead. I looked at him, and all I can say is that I really wanted to shoot him again. I could have just kept going, but there was nothing left except his body. No head, no face. I pulled the burka off, then went into the shower and Angie helped rinse all of him off me, and she helped dry me. I put another one of the burkas on. The ones from the closet. I didn't have the new clothes in there. And that's it. Angie opened the door, Jamie came in to get us, seeing the sheik was dead. We all came out here."

Mike knew why the head was gone. Giving her his small Glock, he had intentionally put hollow point bullets in the gun to be sure it killed him if she was on target or not. That was what that type of bullet did. It wasn't solid. When it entered a body it broke into fragments. It was like shooting a bomb into a body. From that distance, into a head, it combined with the head's internal pressure and shattered it to fly away. With such a shot, such a bullet, Mike worried as they had both seen a true horror. Looking at Cindy, she seemed to appear calm and accepting of what happened. She also seemed glad the man's life had ended while he was using her as a thing he bought — and had no right to in any way. He could only look at her, and nod with admiration. Nodding back, Cindy knew he understood why she felt it was right to do what she had. He looked at each one there.

"Then, it's over. His driver is dead. I shot him the instant he heard the shots and tried to get out with a gun. He travelled with only the driver. I'm sure no other people will come. At least not right now. I'm still concerned with you two seeing what guns can do. It's not a good thing to see. The agency can get you help if it starts troubling you."

Cindy thanked him, saying seeing the man dead stopped what had troubled them. She added it was like waking up from a nightmare. As long as any man thought they were his, it was a nightmare for real."

Then Mike watched something happen to Cindy — and Angie. It was subtle, but he knew neither were the same women he had met just the day before. Thinking about what she had said about waking up from a nightmare, he could see the shot woke Cindy and Angie up. In the planning, they had talked to him about how the only way to stop anyone being taken wasn't by coming to rescue them. Cindy had said the only way to stop trafficking was to stop the traffickers. Dead. She said she would explain in the days ahead, but her mother had stopped the first man who wanted to use her. Her father. It was only when she shot him that he stopped. He would have turned her out like a whore if he had remained alive. She looked at him, and she stared, somehow knowing he understood. She had more to say.

"That man, or boy, or whatever he was. How horrible that he thought he owned us. Mike, Jamie, that will never happen to Angie or me again. I blame myself for letting her go to that audition. Yorgi knew. He warned me. And, wanting so much for something good to be ahead for Angie, I put my own experience of how it works aside, and I even went there with her. We're alive, and we're together. And all of you… I can never tell you how much you mean to me. I'm not stopping with this. I'm not sure how, but I need to stop men like them from doing what they do to anyone. I don't need to ask Angie. She already told me that we need to do everything we can, and we will."

Mike saw the calm and certainty on their faces. He was sure it was trauma. He and Jamie knew it had to be. For now, it was over. They were one of the few who had escaped being trafficked and lost forever.

Saying they needed to go before the sheik was called and then missed, he said the jet was waiting.

Cindy said all they needed to do was to change into regular clothes. Looking around, Cindy asked if they could change on the plane. Saying yes, he said they did have time to change. Cindy looked at him, her brows scrunched in a questioning look.

"Mike… Brian's dead. The sheik's dead. There's nothing more here to do. Let's get going. I'm done here."

Saying goodbye to Yosh and thanking him, she said her mother was impressed he was both big and smart. He laughed, saying it was true, then with the same grin he had when a boy, asked why does a man need to be smart when he can use his muscles. She gave him a punch in his bicep, saying man smart, woman smarter. With that, he smiled and said she just proved it.

Getting into a limo Mike called for, in no time they were in the air, headed home.

Chapter Twenty Two
The Lights of Aurora

On the flight home, Mike knew a lot was yet to happen. He needed to get Jamie a deal and set up with Charles. Cindy and Angie would be debriefed and explain all that had happened once taken to Russia. He had reports to write about why Cindy fired in self-defense, a story they had all sworn to uphold. Knowing he would endure endless ribbing from James about being with Jamie, he couldn't think of a more wonderful thing to be razzed about.

Somehow, four lives had been saved. Cindy, Angie, Jamie, and his own. He knew he wouldn't stop thinking about his sister and where she could be, but he had a new confidence that he would succeed. Or, that he would hear from her.

On the flight back, the most shocking thing since leaving for Russia happened. Asking Cindy about getting her and Angie a safer place to live, he also talked about getting them citizenship. Their help in stopping the trafficking ring was more than an instant deal in his estimation. He knew becoming citizens would be easy, but getting them out of the trailer park to someplace they could afford would not be as easy.

Listening to his concerns, Cindy started laughing. He didn't quite understand how going back to her mobile home could be something to laugh about.

Reminding him she had asked to use his cell phone as they got on the plane, she was worried as she had been gone and there were bills to pay. She wanted to check her bank account then pay anything urgent. She had quietly been sitting across from him, holding the phone as he expressed all his concerns. He asked why she was laughing.

"Well, I'm thinking about how big they make mobile homes.

What do you think about us getting a better one. One with more room, and I sure hope a much better place to put it. Would you have any guess as what that could cost? We do need to get out of there."

She tried not to laugh, but couldn't hold back some giggles.

"Cindy, I have no idea. I'm sure they make some that are all fancy and all, but that would cost a lot of money. Have you thought about a regular house? Brick and mortar? Nice neighborhood?"

"Oh, sure. Mike, that would be so nice. And if we're citizens, we could own land and things. Well, Aurora, it's not too safe. Do you think places in like, Geneva, would cost a lot?"

Not wanting to down her wishful thinking, he said that all depended on how much money it was, and how much she had saved up and things. He asked her how much savings she had. He stopped, then added that maybe with her excellent Russian he could see if the agency had a job for her, which would help her get a mortgage. She put her finger to her lips, thinking hard about what he asked and said.

"Well, I've saved every penny I could. So, before we were, you know, sorry Jamie, taken, I looked at my savings after buying Angie her nice dress, and I was so proud! I've managed to save up $1,150."

Hoping the amount would be much higher, Mike couldn't muster a smile. He sat, slowly shaking his head. She looked worried, and asked him, "Not enough?"

Sadly shaking his head more, he said no, that wouldn't get them far. She nodded, knowing it wouldn't.

"Well, I know it isn't much. But when I looked just a while ago when we got on, I think interest must have been added. Let me log in… yes, here. Mike. Look at my account. Do you think this is fair interest on my savings?"

Handing him his phone, he saw it was her bank account on the screen. It showed her $1,150, then a line for $1.25 in interest, then a deposit for fifty million dollars. It was a wire transfer, not showing where from. He swelled up inside, then showing it to Jamie, she let out a shout of joy. He handed it back to Cindy.

"Your mother?"

She nodded.

"Yes, remember before she hightailed it out of there? When she leaned over to give me a kiss, she asked me where I banked and made sure of the name I was using, which was silly as I only have one name. She said she wanted to make sure we had enough money… For food and other things. So, is this enough for a house in Geneva?"

Jamie put her hand up in front of Mikes mouth as he started to talk. She wanted to answer.

"Cindy. Fuck Geneva! The people there are arrogant assholes. We'll help you find wonderful places and you can visit them all and find one you love."

"Well, I've been thinking about it since I saw the money. Now, I can't pretend. I know where this money comes from… It's all from drugs and taking girls and making them sex workers and things. So, maybe a nice place that's in a nice area for us. I think that we'll need a place like that for some other things, like she said. Food, and other things. I know what those are. Stopping traffickers. Saving girls, just like you saved us is important, and people give money for that. But this money is going to all go to stopping traffickers before they get any girls. Your agency knew about Jamie… oh, Jamie, I'm sorry and its not about you. It's that they knew about you and didn't stop you from taking us. That's the problem and this money can go to doing what agencies like Mike works for aren't doing."

Jamie's eyes lit up and she realized Cindy was right. No agencies or governments had ever tried to stop Brian, or her. It was the other way around. They protected them. She smiled and nodded her head at Cindy.

"See, only someone who's been trafficked could understand. You're right. Nobody tried stopping Brian. The ones running the agencies. The rich guys… And, the ones in office. They opened doors for him. They were his biggest customers. Cindy, you are amazing. I'm with you all the way on it, if you can trust me."

Shaking her head at Jamie, she gave her a classic, "Are you serious?" look.

Then holding her head still as she calmly looked at Jamie, her eyes fixed on hers, she said if she didn't trust her, she'd be dead.

Jamie stopped, then began laughing, growing hysterical.

"If anyone else said that to me, I'd think they'd just be pulling my leg. But, I know for sure that is what I'd be. Wow, good thing I'm actually kind of good down deep inside." She looked at Mike, and they both blushed. Angie asked Cindy why they were blushing, and Cindy said maybe some day she'd explain it to her, but she'd need to be a bit older. She turned to Mike.

"Mike, If money wasn't a concern and you didn't work for the government, would you go with me and Angie, and Jamie now, and stop traffickers? Find your sister?"

Mike looked at her, then broke down, crying for the first time since his sister was gone. Jamie hugged him, and then Cindy and Angie moved to him and hugged him too. He was beyond words.

Jamie rubbed his head, saying they knew that meant yes, and that she was proud he'd be right there with them all.

Cindy nodded, putting her head against Jamie's, then Angie's, and then Mike's. She took a deep breath as she looked into his eyes.

"Okay, then. Mike, I think the first thing we need to do is buy lots of guns and those head popping bullets."

###

About the Author

Author, publisher, photographer and designer, Terry Ulick created the T: Demonic Investigator Series, and Folk Ballads Realized series of novels for Wherever Books.

Publisher of underground newspapers, consumer magazines, books and a glamour photographer, Terry has a career spanning 50 years of creative works including self-help and empowerment books.

An orphan, he learned his family in the Ukraine were drug dealers and sex traffickers, His mother, raped by her ruthless father, escaped to the US where he was born, put in garbage can, found and lived in an orphanage. Eventually finding his mother, he learned the horrific truth of his birth, her escape to America, and how she was trafficked by her own father since a child. His life experiences have shaped his understanding of sex trafficking, and he donates proceeds from his writing to agencies that help stop trafficking, and give care to trafficked women.

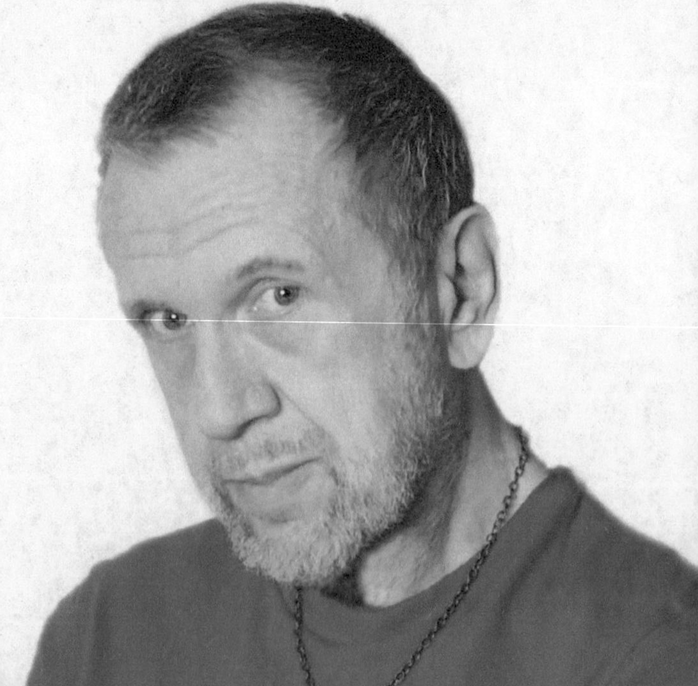

By Terry Ulick

9 7 9 8 9 8 9 2 4 2 5 6 6